DAPHNE

Books by Marilyn Kaye

Max on Earth

Max in Love

Max on Fire

Max Flips Out

DAPHNE

A NOVEL BY

MARILYN KAYE

GULLIVER BOOKS

HARCOURT BRACE JOVANOVICH

SAN DIEGO AUSTIN ORLANDO

Requests for permission to make copies of any part of the work should be mailed to:
Permissions, Harcourt Brace Jovanovich, Publishers, Orlando, Florida 32887.

Library of Congress Cataloging-in-Publication Data
Kaye, Marilyn.
  Daphne.
  "Gulliver books."
  Summary: When shy twelve-year-old Daphne enters junior high school, she has to fight for her own identity as her more outgoing sisters pull her in different directions.
  [1. Identity—Fiction. 2. Sisters—Fiction.
3. Schools—Fiction] I. Title.
PZ7.K2127Dap 1987   [Fic]   86-29420
ISBN 0-15-200434-3
ISBN 0-15-200433-5 (pbk.)

Frontispiece by Roberta Ludlow

Designed by Julie Durrell

Printed in the United States of America

First edition

A B C D E

For Willa Perlman and Sue Cohen

DAPHNE

1

DAPHNE LOVED THE VIEW from her best friend Annie's bedroom window. The trees were so big and leafy they obscured any sign of other houses and she felt like she was in a tree house, right in the middle of a forest. And even if she didn't know what month it was, she could tell the season from those trees. Right now they were whispering of autumn. Some of the leaves had started to turn, and a few had even made a premature trip to the ground.

She adjusted her glasses. Now the view was in clear focus and she could see each individual leaf, separate and distinct. She lowered her head, letting the glasses slip down her nose. Now the leaves were blurry, soft, blending together. She couldn't decide which way was nicer.

"Autumn makes me feel sort of funny inside," she confessed. "Sad, but in a nice kind of way, if you know what I mean."

Annie always knew what she meant. Sitting cross-legged on her bed, she nodded vigorously. "Yeah. I guess you could say it's an ambiguous season."

Daphne looked at her admiringly. What a vocabulary Annie had! And she wasn't showing off, either. Because of that, Daphne didn't hesitate to ask her what *ambiguous* meant.

"It means something has two or more possible meanings. Like, maybe autumn makes you feel sad because it's the end of summer. But you also feel good because it's the beginning of school."

"Ambiguous," Daphne murmured. It was a good word, she thought, storing it away for future use. Not in conversation, of course. She'd feel silly. But maybe in a poem. . . .

"Speaking of school," Annie continued, "can you believe it? In just two more days, we'll be starting junior high. Every time I think about it, I get so excited I feel like I'm going to explode!"

Talk about feeling ambiguous. Daphne shifted uncomfortably. "I guess I'm excited. But it feels weird."

Annie looked thoughtful. "Yeah, I guess it's kind of scary. For one thing, that building's so big I don't know how I'll ever find my way around it. But think about all the good stuff! Did you see there's actually a course called *Poetry?* No grammar! And there's a creative writing club, too."

Daphne's forehead puckered. "You mean where people sit around and write poems and stories and stuff?"

"I don't think that's how it works. You probably write stuff at home, then bring it to meetings and read it to the others."

Daphne shuddered. She couldn't imagine sharing her writing with anyone but Annie. Oh, sometimes she showed poems to her parents or her sisters, but to total strangers? Those odd little poems, her own private thoughts, those funny little feelings she had in her heart—could other seventh graders possibly understand? Would she even want to find out?

"I think it'll be interesting meeting other people who like to write," Annie continued. "Don't you?"

"I guess," Daphne said. Actually, to see what other people were writing would be very interesting. Showing them her own stuff was another matter altogether.

"Well, one thing's for sure—junior high's going to be a lot different from elementary school," Annie said with satisfaction.

This time Daphne could agree wholeheartedly. "Cassie says everything's really different in junior high."

Annie looked at her with interest. "Oh, yeah? Like what?"

Daphne tried to recall exactly what her sister had been chattering about over the past few weeks. "Well, you have different teachers for each subject, and you don't stay in the same room like we did in elementary school."

"I like that," Annie said happily. "It won't be so boring. And then if we get some teachers we don't like, at least we won't be stuck with them all day. Remember Mrs. Schultz?"

Daphne made a face. "She was awful. Remember that time you passed me a note and she caught us and made us stand in front of the whole class and read it out loud?" The memory, three years later, could still make her face go red with shame.

"I guess the classes will be a lot harder, too," Annie mused. "And there'll be a lot more homework."

Daphne nodded. "Cassie's always complaining about how much work she has to do." She paused. "Of course, she was always complaining in elementary school, too."

"Yeah, you two are really different. Sometimes I can't believe you're actually sisters." Just then the phone rang, and Annie jumped off her bed. "I'd better go get that." She ran out of the room, leaving Daphne alone with her thoughts.

She *was* very different from Cassie. But then, all her sisters were different, from her and from each other. There was beautiful Cassandra, just one year older than Daphne, but so much more sophisticated. She went to parties, had lots of friends, and knew how to talk to boys.

Then there was Lydia, the oldest. She'd be a ninth grader this fall. And while Cassie liked to do what all her friends were doing, Lydia always wanted to be different. She didn't care about fashion or gossip or any of those things their mother referred to as "typically adolescent." Their father called Lydia a free spirit.

Finally, there was Phoebe, the youngest. Daphne figured she was closest to Fee, mainly because they shared a bedroom. But Fee was different, too—friendly, easygoing, and not a bit shy.

None of them even looked like the others. Daphne got off the bed and wandered over to the mirror hanging over Annie's dresser. Well, she didn't have Cassie's looks, that was for sure. The solemn face that stared back at her would never be called beautiful. She tried to look at her reflection objectively. Dark, deep-set eyes under her glasses, a nose that seemed to go off to the right a bit, thin lips, dark hair that was just hair—straight and fine and hanging just below her chin.

"What are you looking at?"

Daphne hadn't even heard Annie come back in. She grinned self-consciously. "Just trying to decide what I look like."

Annie cocked her head to one side and eyed her critically. "You look . . . interesting. Interesting and artistic. Like a poet."

Daphne turned back to the mirror. Artistic. Well, that wasn't bad. The reflection smiled back at her.

"What about me?" Annie asked. "What do I look like?"

Daphne scrutinized her best friend. Annie had reddish brown frizzy curls that seemed to go off in all directions, a space between her two front teeth, and lots of freckles. No, Annie wasn't beautiful either.

"Intellectual," Daphne pronounced. "Interesting. *And* artistic."

Annie seemed satisfied with that. "You know, I don't think I'd want to be beautiful like Cassie. Too many problems."

"I know," Daphne agreed. "Cassie's always putting goo on her face and rolling her hair, and she's forever on a diet." She turned back to the mirror and touched her own hair. "Do you think I should get my hair cut?"

"Do you *want* to get your hair cut?" Annie asked pointedly.

Daphne shook her head. "Not really. But Cassie keeps telling me I should get it cut. She says now that I'm in junior high I should start paying more attention to my appearance."

"Why?"

Daphne sighed. "I think that's the sort of thing she's talking about when she says everything's different in junior high."

"Hair?"

"Not just hair. Cassie says it's really important to look right—you know, clothes, and hairstyles, and . . ."

Annie's forehead wrinkled. "Really? When I go by the school, I see a lot of kids wearing jeans, just like we did in elementary school."

"Oh, Cassie says jeans are okay," Daphne assured her. "But not all the time. And she says they can't be just any jeans. Cassie says this year everyone's wearing What jeans."

"What jeans?"

Daphne nodded.

Annie frowned and repeated, "What jeans?"

"Yeah."

Her friend groaned in exasperation. "Why won't you answer me?"

"I did!"

Annie stared at her. "I asked you what kind of jeans?"

Daphne stared back. Then she started laughing. "That's the name of them—*What* jeans. It's a brand, I guess."

"Huh?" Annie shook her head. "I don't get it. Jeans are jeans."

"That's what I told Cassie. But she says you have to have jeans that say *What* on the back pocket."

Annie rolled her eyes. "No offense, Daphne, but that's the dumbest thing I ever heard. What do the T-shirts have to say—*Why?*"

Daphne's eyes twinkled. "Right—and the socks have to say *Who*."

Annie grinned. "What about *When* and *Where?*"

Daphne cocked her head to one side. "I guess you'd have to wear gloves."

Both girls cracked up.

"What else does Cassie say?" Annie said between fits of giggling.

"Let me think. . . . Well, she says it's important to hang out with the right people."

"How do you know who the right people are?"

Daphne's lips twitched. "I guess they're the ones with the What jeans."

Annie started laughing again. "I can see it all now. We'll walk into school that first day in our plain old Levi's and there'll be a guard at the entrance. And he'll take one look at our jeans, call out the entire security force—"

"—and throw us right out the door," Daphne finished. This picture set them off into another fit of giggles.

"Hey, I'm hungry," Annie managed to choke out. "Let's go see if there's anything to eat."

Daphne followed her downstairs to the kitchen. "Cassie keeps telling me about all the cliques in junior high. She says practically everybody's in a clique."

Annie opened the refrigerator door and perused the contents. "What kind of cliques?"

Daphne tried to remember exactly what Cassie had said. "Well, there are the popular kids, and there are the nerds, and the brains. . . ."

Annie pulled out a pie tin, handed it to Daphne, and reached back in for a carton of milk. "I guess we could be brains."

"I don't know," Daphne said, peeking under the aluminum foil for a look at the pie. "She says the brains are the ones who look terribly serious and raise their hands in class all the time and never have any fun."

"Well, I guess we wouldn't fit in there." Annie got glasses and plates and forks, and the two settled down at the kitchen table. "You hardly ever raise your hand in class. And I don't either, much."

That was true, Daphne thought. She was too shy, and Annie . . . Annie never thought she knew the right answer, even when she did.

Annie examined the chunk of pie on her fork. "So we're not brains. I don't think we're nerds, are we?"

"Oh, no—definitely not nerds," Daphne agreed. "But I don't think we'll fit in with the popular crowd either. Those are the kids like Cassie."

Her mouth full, Annie could only manage a vigorous nod. She swallowed, then asked, "What's left? If we're not popular or nerds or brains, what are we?"

"I asked Cassie that. She said if you're not in a clique, you're a nobody."

Annie looked thoughtful. "I guess we'll be nobodies then. But at least we'll be nobodies together."

The girls concentrated on their pie and ate in silence for a few moments.

"What about Lydia?" Annie asked suddenly. "She doesn't fit into any of those categories either. What clique is Lydia in?"

Daphne thought for a few seconds. "I don't think Lydia's in a clique. But she's definitely not a nobody either."

"What does she say about junior high?"

Daphne drained the last of her milk. "She hasn't said much at all lately—to anyone. She wants to be made the school newspaper editor this fall, and she's been working on this paper she has to turn in, writing out her goals and objectives and all that stuff. She's been holed up in her room this entire week." Daphne contemplated her empty glass. "I can't picture Lydia in a clique. She likes to be different. My dad says Lydia's a leader and Cassie's a follower."

"What are we?"

"I don't know."

"Not leaders," Annie murmured.

"No, absolutely not leaders," Daphne agreed.

"But we're not followers either. Remember last year when all the girls in the sixth grade were wearing those lacy bows in their hair and we thought they looked dumb? We were practically the only ones *not* wearing bows."

Daphne nodded. She never could see the point of doing something just because everyone else was doing it. On the other hand, she didn't think she'd like being *too* different, like Lydia.

"We're not leaders and we're not followers," Annie continued. "I guess whatever we are doesn't have a name."

"I'm going to ask Lydia about it. As soon as she finishes this newspaper thing."

Where would they fit in? she wondered. She got up and walked over to the kitchen window. Special jeans. Cliques. Creative writing clubs. Cedar Park Junior High was going to be very, very different from Eastside Elementary. What if she did something really dumb or said something really stupid—and everyone looked at her and laughed? Or what if she got lost the very first day and couldn't find her classroom?

With all the mental strength she could muster, Daphne pushed these frightening thoughts from her mind. She had *sisters.* Cassie and Lydia wouldn't let her make any awful mistakes.

Annie broke into her thoughts. "You know what my

mom said? She said junior high's a time to find out who we are and what we're really like. I think that's exciting, don't you?"

Daphne agreed—sort of. She wondered who *she'd* be like—Cassie or Lydia? Maybe she'd be a little like both—after all, how could a person choose between sisters?

Annie was right. It *was* an exciting time. And yes, Daphne was definitely excited. But she was something else, too. Scared.

2

OPENING THE BACK DOOR of the white frame house, Daphne was greeted by familiar sounds, each immediately identifiable. From the living room came the noise of a blaring television, canned laughter mixed with human giggles. That would be Fee—with Linn, Jessica, or Melanie—glued to reruns of "Leave It to Beaver." Wafting down from the second story came strains of Bruce Springsteen accompanied by the clacking of typewriter keys—that had to be Lydia. Slightly closer, from the upstairs hallway, came a shrill squeal: "Did he *really?* What did you tell him?" Definitely Cassie.

There was another voice too, more like a mumble, coming from the tiny room off the kitchen. It had been a pantry, but ever since the canned goods were replaced by books and a small desk, it was called the study. Daphne peeked inside.

Her mother was leaning back in her chair, feet propped on the desk, her eyes closed and her lips moving. Daphne could just barely make out the words.

"So if you think Shakespeare's just some ancient dead writer, you're wrong. Believe it or not, Shakespeare's got a lot to say to young people today."

"Mom?"

Mrs. Gray opened her eyes, blinked, and then smiled. "I'm practicing for the first day of school. What do you think of this?" She grabbed some sheets of paper from the desk and read out loud.

" 'I think you kids just might relate to Romeo and Juliet. You guys might even pick up some tips from Romeo—but only if your sweetie has a balcony!' " She punctuated this with a perky smile, paused, and looked up at Daphne anxiously. "Well?"

Daphne wanted to be kind. "It's okay, Mom. I guess."

Her mother's face fell. "You don't like it."

Daphne chose her words carefully. "It's not that I don't like it, exactly—it just doesn't sound like you."

Mrs. Gray sighed. "I know. I just thought if I made some jokes . . ."

"Just be yourself, Mom. You don't have to make any jokes."

Her mother laughed. "I feel like I'm the child and you're the mother! Honestly, Daphne, I think I'm more nervous about teaching school than you are about starting junior high."

13

"I'm nervous too, Mom."

Mrs. Gray gave her a sympathetic look. "I know, honey. You've never been crazy about new experiences. But remember, you've got two sisters to watch over you and help you out. They must be giving you lots of advice."

"Cassie has."

"What about Lydia? Have you talked to her?"

"Talk to Lydia about what?" The tall, lanky, short-haired figure in the doorway looked flushed and excited. Without waiting for an answer to her first question, she asked another. "Is Dad home yet?"

"Any minute now. What's up?"

Lydia waved some neatly typed papers in the air. "I finished my statement of purpose."

"Your what?" Mrs. Gray asked.

"My statement of purpose. It's what we have to submit to be considered for editor of the *Cedar Century*. I want to get Dad's opinion."

Mrs. Gray looked mildly offended. "Not mine?"

Lydia was oblivious to her mother's tone. "Oh, if you want to read it, sure. But Dad's a real newspaper editor. He knows a lot more about this kind of thing than you do."

Daphne winced. Lydia always said exactly what she thought. And even though she sort of admired that, sometimes she wondered if Lydia ever realized she might be hurting someone's feelings.

Mrs. Gray was used to the way Lydia talked, but still looked a bit miffed. "Well, I'm an English teacher—or at least, I will be in two days. I think I just might know something about good writing."

Her injured tone actually managed to penetrate Lydia's consciousness. "Sorry, Mom. I didn't mean to sound like I didn't want your opinion. I was just thinking about Dad. . . ."

Mrs. Gray shook her head in amusement. "Your father may be editor, but guess who checks his editorials for language and style?"

Lydia's eyebrows went up. "Oh, yeah?" She thrust the pages toward her. "Okay, you want to read this?"

Their mother grinned. "I will, dear—later. Right now I've got to get dinner started. Whose turn is it to help tonight?"

"Cassie's," Lydia said. "She's on the phone."

"What a surprise," Mrs. Gray murmured. "Sometimes I think that phone's become an extension of her body. Guess I'll just have to go perform a little major surgery." She paused at the door. "Lydia, why don't you talk to Daphne about starting junior high?"

Lydia was studying her paper. "Huh? Oh, yeah—sure, Mom." She smiled brightly at Daphne. "Want to read my statement of purpose?"

"Sure," Daphne replied, taking the sheets from her. "But I don't know any more about editing a newspaper than Mom does."

"That's okay," Lydia assured her. "I'm just interested in your opinion of my writing style. You don't have to pay any attention to what I'm actually saying."

That wasn't easy. Lydia's statement of purpose sounded

more like a declaration of war. Sentences leaped off the page.

"Students at Cedar Park Junior High are uninformed, passive, and uncommitted. They are in desperate need of a newspaper that presents major issues, a newspaper that challenges them and incites them to action. There are serious problems at this school. My *Cedar Century* would point out these problems and bring them to the attention of students, forcing them to take a stand," Daphne read silently. Her eyes widened.

"Wow," she whispered. "What's going on at that school? What are these serious problems?"

Lydia made a sweeping gesture. "Oh, there are tons of them. Like this stupid Miss Cedar Park Junior Princess contest—have you ever heard of anything so sexist? And they have these ridiculous rules about clothes."

"What kind of rules?" Surely they couldn't require What jeans. . . .

The scorn on Lydia's face was unmistakable. "They won't let us wear T-shirts with messages on them. You know that great T-shirt I have, the one that says 'A woman without a man is like a fish without a bicycle'?"

Daphne nodded.

"Well, I wore it one day last spring, and my creepy homeroom teacher made me go into the restroom and turn it inside out. I had to wear it like that all day!"

Daphne shuddered, making a mental note not to wear any T-shirts with messages on them.

"There's a lot of stuff wrong with that place," Lydia

16

said darkly. "And I've only got one more year to try to make some changes." Then she brightened. "But at least I'll have you to follow in my footsteps."

"Huh?" Daphne was caught off guard.

"Once I'm editor of the newspaper, I'll put you on the staff. What do you like best—features or editorials or straight news?"

"Lydia, I don't know anything about newspapers!"

Lydia waved that aside. "You like to write, don't you?"

"Poems," Daphne said. "I write poems and stories—those sorts of things."

"Writing's writing," Lydia stated flatly. "Hey, you might even be editor yourself someday!"

"Me? An editor? I don't think—"

But Lydia didn't let her finish. "I hear Dad! I'd better go catch him before dinner." She must have caught a glimpse of Daphne's expression, though, because she stopped and patted her younger sister's shoulder comfortingly.

"Listen, don't worry about junior high, okay? I'll be there, and I'll point you in all the right directions." Then she ran out, calling over her shoulder, "And don't listen to anything Cassie says!"

"You girls all ready for school on Monday?" Mr. Gray asked jovially as he passed the cake plates.

"No," Cassie replied succinctly, wrinkling her nose for added emphasis. Her nose remained wrinkled as she examined the slice of cake on her plate. "Is this homemade?"

Mrs. Gray gave her "the look." "No, it is not home-made. I told you girls: now that I'm going back to teaching full-time, I'm not going to be baking like I used to."

Cassie didn't look too perturbed. "Well, I wasn't going to eat it anyway. Too fattening."

Lydia threw in her two cents. "I'm more than willing to give up homemade cakes so Mom can be a liberated woman."

Mrs. Gray looked at her oldest daughter with a combination of amusement and approval. "I'm truly appreciative of your support, Lydia. And I know you'll be just as gracious in taking on a few extra chores around the house."

Lydia's face fell and Fee giggled.

"What about you, pumpkin?" Mr. Gray asked Phoebe. "Are you looking forward to school?"

"Absolutely," Fee said. She pushed a strand of hair out of her eyes and beamed happily. "Sixth graders rule the school! Me and Linn and Jess and Mel are going to be hall monitors and push the little kids around. Boy, am I ready for that!"

For a fleeting moment, Daphne envied her little sister, returning to the safe, secure world of Eastside Elementary where nobody cared what kind of jeans you wore.

"I'm not ready," Mrs. Gray sighed. "To tell you the truth, I'm scared stiff. What if the kids don't like me?"

"Of course they'll like you," Mr. Gray said staunchly.

"I don't know," Lydia said thoughtfully. "They might not."

A chorus of voices exclaimed, "Lydia!"

"Well, I'm just being realistic. I mean, some kids just hate teachers, period. No matter how nice they are."

"I think Mom's going to be a great teacher," Daphne said quickly. "Even if those kids don't like other teachers, they'll like you, Mom."

"I liked a teacher once," Cassie mused. "She wore these great silk shirts, and her shoes always matched her skirt."

Mr. Gray nodded solemnly. "An excellent reason to admire a teacher. What about you, Daphne? Looking forward to starting a new school?"

Daphne hoped she sounded more confident than she felt. "Annie says there's a creative writing club. I think that could be neat."

Cassie looked at her quizzically. "I've never heard of that. Lydia, do you know anything about a creative writing club?"

"I think I've heard of it. But I don't think they do anything important."

Mr. Gray raised his eyebrows. "That's a subjective comment. Maybe *you* don't think what they do is important, but Daphne might."

Lydia and Cassie only shrugged, but Daphne eyed her father gratefully. That was just what she'd wanted to say—but she didn't want to start an argument.

"I think a creative writing club could be great fun," Mrs. Gray said. "It sounds like something just right for Daphne."

Daphne nodded fervently and looked at Lydia and

Cassie to see their reactions. But they had begun debating the pros and cons of signing up for volleyball in phys ed and weren't even listening.

"Are you going to miss Eastside?" Fee asked later. She took the last dish from Daphne's soapy hands and started drying it.

"A little," Daphne admitted.

"But think of all the new kids you'll meet in junior high," Fee said. "Won't that be exciting?"

Daphne contemplated the prospect. "For you, maybe. I'm a lot shyer than you are."

"That's true," Fee said cheerfully. "We're pretty different people—we all are."

Daphne nodded in agreement. Each of them was unique, her mother always said. Like snowflakes. Or like the leaves on the trees . . . when she had her glasses on.

She was on her way to her room when Cassie cornered her in the hallway. "Have you picked out what you're going to wear for the first day of school?"

Daphne hadn't even given the matter any thought at all. "It's only Friday, Cassie! I don't need two days to lay out my clothes!"

Cassie put her hands on her hips, eyeing her sternly. "What you wear on the first day is *very* important. Come on, let's go through your closet and see what you've got."

Daphne obediently followed her older sister into the bedroom. Cassie threw open the closet doors and began briskly going through the clothes hanging on Daphne's side. "This is awful . . . nobody's wearing pointed collars . . . this isn't too bad . . . if you shorten this skirt, you might be able to get away with it."

"I thought I'd just wear my jeans," Daphne offered tentatively. She knew what Cassie was going to say, and quickly added, "I know they're not *What* jeans, but I could wear a long shirt and no one would see the label."

"I guess that would do," Cassie said, but with a definite lack of conviction. Then her voice softened. "Look, Daphne, I know it sounds like I'm making a big fuss about all this. But it's so important to make a good impression. I'm doing this for you! I want you to be happy and have a good time in junior high, just like me."

Daphne tried to look appreciative. She reminded herself how lucky she was to have a sister who cared about her.

"If you just listen to me," Cassie continued, "I'll tell you everything you need to know to be a big hit in school. I'll get you in with the popular kids, show you what clubs to join—everything!"

"Thanks, Cassie."

Cassie smiled benignly. "It's no problem. Remember, when you walk into that school, people are going to say 'She's Cassie Gray's sister!' You know, you're really lucky I'm here to tell you everything you need to know."

"And Annie, too," Daphne added.

"Oh, sure," Cassie said. "I'll tell Annie what to do."

Well, that was a relief. Despite what Lydia had said to her, she would listen to Cassie. She'd listen to both of them. Then she couldn't possibly end up being a nobody or looking like a jerk.

Feeling more cheerful, Daphne headed out to the hall to call Annie. Her parents' bedroom door was open, and she couldn't help but overhear their conversation.

"Did you read that statement of purpose Lydia wrote about her plans for editing the school paper?"

Mr. Gray chuckled. "Is that what it was? It sounded more like a plan to overthrow the government."

"Oh, dear. What did you tell her?"

"Well, I suggested she tone it down a bit, make it sound a little less revolutionary."

"Will she?" Mrs. Gray asked.

"I doubt it. You know our Lydia—when she's made up her mind about something, she sticks to it. Once she's on a campaign, there's no stopping her."

That was Lydia all right, Daphne thought. She dialed Annie's number.

"Hi, it's me. Guess what? I talked to Lydia and Cassie, and they both said they're going to watch out for us at school and tell us what to do."

"I guess that's good," Annie said slowly. "But what if we don't want to do what they tell us to?"

"Oh, come on, Annie—they want to help us! I think we're lucky."

Annie didn't sound very enthusiastic. "Well, okay. I'll see ya tomorrow."

Daphne hung up the phone. They *were* lucky, she and Annie, and Annie would realize it once they started school. At least they weren't going to be nobodies. Cassie and Lydia would see to that.

3

DAPHNE CLUTCHED the three-ringed note-book to her chest and pressed herself as tightly as possible against the wall. Her eyes swept over the crush of people surging into the large entrance hallway. The area had seemed much larger the day she'd come to register. Now, crowded with yelling, laughing, waving junior high school students, it was cramped and confusing. Would she ever find Annie?

She had managed to wedge herself into a space next to the trophy case where she could see everyone but no one would notice her. She glanced at the big black-and-white clock that hung over the entranceway—8:29. Annie should be there in exactly one minute.

She scanned the faces. Here and there she spotted a

familiar one, a classmate from Eastside. But for the most part the room was a blur—a sea of strangers. And there were so many of them.

The crowd seemed to be moving in one solid mass, heading for the various corridors that led to the classrooms. But more people were coming in the door. It was like an endless stream.

Daphne thought she heard her name. She looked up. Was that tall, fair-haired girl waving at her? Oh, yes—it was Martha Jane, Lydia's friend. Daphne smiled brightly, waved back, and pretended to be studying the contents of the trophy case. State Debate Finals, Second Place, 1982. Girls' Tennis, Regional Championship, 1984. Semifinals, Cross Country, 1985.

She looked at the clock again—8:32. Where was Annie? Once more Daphne searched the faces. She noticed a girl looking directly at her, and dropped her eyes. All those feet—maybe she'd recognize Annie's red sneakers.

"Aren't you Cassie's sister?"

Daphne's head jerked up. A pretty, curly-haired girl in a denim jacket was edging through the crowd toward her.

"You're Daphne, right?"

Daphne smiled shyly and nodded.

"I'm Alison—remember me?"

Daphne managed to nod again while she racked her brain. Cassie had so many friends.

"Why are you hanging around here? Can't you find your homeroom? Let me see your schedule."

She grabbed the piece of paper Daphne was clutching and looked at it. "D-14. C'mon, I'll show you where it is." She grabbed Daphne's arm and started to pull her away.

"I'm waiting for someone," Daphne protested weakly. Frantically, she scanned the crowd again. And suddenly, there was Annie, her red curls bobbing wildly as she weaved through the crowd.

"Daphne!"

Daphne extricated herself from Alison's grasp, smiled apologetically, and murmured, "Excuse me, there's my friend." She must have said a dozen more excuse me's before she finally reached Annie.

"There you are! I thought you were going to be late!"

"I think it took me ten minutes just to get through the door," Annie gasped breathlessly. "Can you believe all these people?"

The girls allowed themselves to get pushed forward with the crowd. Daphne gazed in bewilderment at the corridors leading off the main hallway. "How do we know which way to go?" Thank goodness she and Annie had the same homeroom assignment! At least if they were going to get lost, they'd get lost together.

The crowd started to thin as students took off down the various hallways.

"Should we ask someone which way to go?" Annie asked.

Daphne really didn't want to. She searched the hallway for some clue. . . . "There!" she exclaimed triumphantly.

Sure enough, each corridor had a letter over its entrance, and one of them was *D*. The girls hurried down the hallway, where students were drifting into rooms or pausing to chat in front of open doors. They kept their eyes glued to the numbers above the doors.

"D-9 . . . D-11 . . . it must be on the other side," Annie said. "There it is!"

With some trepidation, Daphne followed Annie into the room. It was almost full of seventh graders, some looking just as uneasy as she knew she did.

"There's Carol Harrison from Eastside," Annie whispered. "And Bobby Ellis."

Even though neither had ever been particularly good friends of theirs, they greeted each other with enthusiasm. Daphne figured they were all feeling the same way—just happy to see a familiar face.

Annie pointed to two seats in the back and the girls made their way there. Safely settled in her seat, Daphne had a chance to look around.

She couldn't believe there were so many twelve-year-olds in Cedar Park—and this was only one homeroom. Except for Carol and Bobby, she didn't think she'd ever even seen any of these kids before. Of course, there were eight elementary schools in Cedar Park, so she wouldn't know kids from anyplace but Eastside. And she'd only know the ones from her own class—there had been two other sixth-grade classes at Eastside. She didn't even know the ones from her own class that well.

Daphne practically jumped out of her seat as a shrill

ringing resounded through the room. At the same time, a handsome man in a blue suit entered with a stack of papers and books. He dropped them on the desk in front of the room.

"Good morning. I'm Mr. Hudson, and I'll be your homeroom teacher this year," he announced.

Daphne and Annie exchanged wide-eyed looks. They'd never had a man for a teacher before.

"I hope to learn all your names soon," Mr. Hudson continued. "When I call the role, please let me know if I'm making a total mess out of your name. Or you might have some sort of nickname—like Madman or Killer. Let me know your preference, and I'll make every effort to remember it." He winked at the class. "I probably won't—but I'll try."

He had just finished going through the names when there was a sound of three bells from the intercom. This was followed by a short blast of static, and then a hollow voice.

"May I have your attention for the morning announcements? This is your principal, Dr. Spaulding. On behalf of the faculty and staff at Cedar Park Junior High School, I welcome you all to the first day of the school year. A special welcome goes out to all you seventh graders. We wish you a happy and productive three years.

"Now for the announcements. Class elections will be held in two weeks. Students wishing to run for class office may sign up in the main office or at the Extracurricular Fair. The Extracurricular Fair will be held this afternoon in the cafeteria, immediately following the last class period."

"That's where we can sign up for the Creative Writing Club," Annie whispered to Daphne.

When the announcements were over, Mr. Hudson addressed the class again. "I have several forms here for you to fill out. I know that's a drag, but while you're doing it, I'll entertain you with my standard first-day-of-school pep talk. Just do me one favor: try not to snore loudly while I'm talking."

With the rest of the class, Daphne laughed. If all the teachers were like Mr. Hudson, junior high might actually be fun.

His "pep talk" wasn't boring at all. He talked about the new experiences they were going to have, the challenges, and how they weren't elementary school babies anymore. He said they'd be making some of their own decisions, taking on more responsibilities, that sort of thing. As he spoke, Daphne actually felt a shiver of excitement run through her.

When the bell rang signalling the end of homeroom, she turned to Annie. "He's neat!"

Annie's eyes were bright. "Yeah, I think so, too. None of the teachers at Eastside ever made jokes like that."

The two girls had to separate then—Annie had math and Daphne had history. But the feeling Mr. Hudson's talk had given her lasted, and Daphne made her way alone to the next class with something almost like confidence. Not quite—but almost.

The history teacher turned out to be one who had

been there for a long time. While she was calling the role, she occasionally stopped to ask a student if he or she was so-and-so's brother or sister. She paused when she reached Daphne's name.

"Are you Lydia Gray's sister?"

Daphne hoped she wasn't blushing. "Yes," she replied softly.

"And Cassie Gray's your sister, too."

This was more a statement than a question, but Daphne felt like she had to say something, so she just whispered yes again. The teacher looked at her keenly. Daphne felt warm all over. She wasn't sure she liked the attention—but at least she wasn't a nobody.

After history came science. Daphne approached the class with slightly more anxiety. She'd never been very good in science, and the teacher looked very stern. She wished Annie was sitting next to her. The girl in the next chair seemed very serious, with dark-rimmed glasses and long, straight dark hair pulled back with plain barrettes. Probably a brain, Daphne decided.

After class, she was surprised when the girl turned to her with a grin. "This is gonna be great! Science classes in elementary school were so dippy."

Her smile was so infectious Daphne found herself grinning back. "I'm terrible in science," she admitted.

"Maybe we can work together," the girl offered. "I'm Barbara Goldman."

"I'm Daphne Gray."

"What a pretty name! See ya tomorrow."

Maybe science wouldn't be so bad after all, Daphne

thought as she walked down the hall to the gymnasium for phys ed. Entering the gym, she joined the group sitting on the bleachers. She'd signed up for gymnastics, but since this was the first day, they didn't have to do anything. The teacher gave them instructions on getting gym clothes, showed them where the lockers and showers were, and then talked to them about what they'd be doing the next day.

But when Daphne left the gym, she panicked. It was her lunch period—and she didn't have the slightest idea where the cafeteria was.

Ask someone, she told herself sternly. But the thought of stopping one of those figures dashing by in pairs and groups made her stomach churn.

She chose a hallway at random and hurried down it, but it only led to another hallway. She ran down that one, but it ended in a dead end. She ran back the way she'd come, feeling like a mouse in a maze and on the verge of tears.

Then she caught a bit of conversation between two boys walking alongside her.

"I'm starving."

"Yeah—me, too."

She followed them closely, up a flight of stairs and down another hall. Then suddenly she was in a huge room that reminded her of the scene in the entrance hallway that morning—only more so.

Surely the entire school couldn't be having lunch at the same time! But that's what it looked like—masses of kids clutching trays and lunch bags, yelling at each other "Over here!" "Get me a milk, would you?" or "Hey, that seat's saved!"

Daphne stood there, frozen. There was a long line off to one side—that had to be where you got the lunch. But what if she made a mistake and sat in a seat that was saved? She'd die, she'd just die.

And she'd never find Annie in this crowd! They'd told each other they'd meet in the cafeteria for lunch— but who would have guessed it would be such a zoo?

Daphne made her way to the line. It moved quickly, and before long she found herself standing frozen again, this time with a tray of unidentifiable mush that vaguely resembled food.

Where should she sit? How was she supposed to know where to go?

"Daphne! Over here!"

She didn't think she'd ever been so happy to see Cassie before. Waves of relief poured over her as she moved swiftly to the table where her sister was waving to her.

"Sit down! You know Barbie."

Daphne said hello to the girl sitting across from her.

"And this is Barbie's sister, Kimmie. She's in seventh grade, too."

A petite girl with light-brown hair in a stylish cut said, "Hi! Isn't this great? Not like elementary school, where the teachers eat with you. I love this place!"

"It's different," Daphne admitted. Then she saw Annie, holding a brown bag and searching the room. Daphne jumped up. "Annie!" she called.

Annie lit up when she saw her and came over. Daphne introduced her to Barbie and Kimmie, and Annie sat down.

Kimmie was eyeing Annie's bag curiously. "Is that your lunch?"

"Yeah. Tuna fish sandwiches. Want one?"

Kimmie didn't answer. Instead she turned to her sister. "You told me *nobody* brings lunches."

Barbie didn't say anything. She just eyed the brown bag and then exchanged glances with Cassie.

Daphne turned to *her* sister. "But you're always saying how awful the cafeteria food is!"

"Oh, it *is*," Cassie assured her. "But we all get it anyway." She smiled kindly at Annie. "Don't bring your lunch anymore, Annie. Brown bags are just so . . . you know, *elementary school.*"

Annie pondered her brown bag. "Well, at least it's not a Mickey Mouse lunch box!" she said cheerfully.

Cassie and Barbie exchanged another look. "We were just telling Kimmie about how we do things in junior high," Barbie said. "You know—what's cool, what's not."

Kimmie turned to Daphne enthusiastically. "This is going to keep us from making any dumb mistakes. We're so lucky to have older sisters here!"

Daphne nodded vigorously. If Cassie hadn't been there, she might still be wandering around the room with the tray in her hands.

"Like, this morning I almost put a barrette in my hair. Barbie caught me just in time. She says *nobody* wears barrettes in their hair."

A picture flashed through Daphne's mind. "There was a girl sitting next to me in science who had a barrette in her hair. Two, in fact."

Cassie made a face. "She's probably a nerd."

Daphne glanced at Annie. Her friend was busily consuming her sandwich and appeared to be only half-listening. Or at least she hadn't made any effort to remove the barrette that was ineffectually holding some curls out of her eyes.

"We're going to keep an eye on you guys at the Extracurricular Fair this afternoon," Cassie said.

Daphne was happy to hear that. She suspected the scene in the gym would be just as crazy and confusing as this one.

"We have to make sure you don't join any of the wrong clubs," Barbie said. "Like the Science Club, for example." She made a face. "They're all nerds."

Well, there was no fear of that, as far as Daphne was concerned.

Annie looked up. "Do you know about the Creative Writing Club?"

Barbie looked at her blankly. "Never heard of it."

Kimmie wrinkled her nose. "That sounds more like a class than a club. I thought the clubs were supposed to be fun."

"Where's Lydia?" Daphne asked.

"She has a later lunch period," Cassie replied. "Now look, Daphne—don't let her try to get you involved in any of her crazy stuff."

"What kind of crazy stuff? Like the newspaper?"

"Oh, the newspaper's okay, I guess," Cassie said. "But stay away from all that political stuff she's into, like starting petitions and all that."

"I don't think that's my kind of thing," Daphne murmured.

"Sounds really nerdy," Kimmie said.

Annie was looking at Cassie curiously. "Do you think Lydia's a nerd?"

"Of course not!" Cassie exclaimed. "She's my sister!"

"It's just that sometimes she does things that make people think she's a nerd," Barbie said.

Once lunch was over, Annie and Daphne took off for English, the only other class they had together and the one Daphne was most looking forward to. They found seats together, and Daphne saw Annie beckon to a boy to join them.

"Daphne, this is Jerry. He's in my math class." She laughed. "We discovered this morning that we both hate math."

"So we knew we were going to be friends," Jerry said.

Daphne turned a puzzled eye to Annie. She hadn't said anything about making a friend.

"Daphne's not crazy about math, either," Annie offered. "But we both like English."

"Me, too," Jerry said happily.

"Good morning, class," said a pretty, young woman standing up front. "I'm Ms. McBain."

Daphne focused on the teacher, who had just started to take roll. But her mind was reeling. She'd gone from feeling anxious to okay to panicky to better—and now

Annie had found a new friend. Furtively, Daphne looked him over. He was kind of short, with light-brown hair and regular trousers—not blue jeans. If he was Annie's friend, he'd have to be her friend, too.

She just hoped he wasn't a nerd.

4

WHEN THE LAST BELL RANG, Daphne gathered her books and headed for the cafeteria. She was able to find it this time without any difficulty and that gave her a good feeling—like she was starting to know her way around. And three people had said hello to her on the way—a friend of Lydia's, Cassie's friend Barbie, and a girl who'd sat next to her in math. That gave her an extra lift. Funny—just a few hours before, the place had seemed like a frightening, bewildering maze. Now it almost felt comfortable.

This time, she and Annie had wisely arranged to meet at a specific spot—down and across the hall, in front of the clinic.

Daphne got there first. From her vantage point, she

could see hordes of kids pouring into the cafeteria. It was the third time she'd faced the same scene—but this time the crowd didn't look nearly as scary as it had that morning. She even recognized a few faces from her classes. They were beginning to look less like a mob and more like a crowd of individual people.

She shifted a load of books from one arm to the other, and groaned slightly at their weight. Just then the door to the clinic opened. A woman in a white dress eyed her eagerly.

"Aren't you feeling well, dear? Come in, come in."

Daphne gulped. "Oh, no—I'm fine." The woman didn't look convinced, so she hastily added, "Really—I'm okay. I'm just waiting for a friend."

The woman seemed almost disappointed. "You kids are so healthy," she said. "I haven't had one patient all day." She smiled at Daphne and then retreated back into the room.

Daphne looked at the closed door sympathetically. Poor woman. It must be lonely in there. Maybe later in the term she'd fake a sniffle. . . .

"Daphne!"

Annie bustled down the hall toward her. She was accompanied by Jerry.

"That English class is great," he said enthusiastically. "I already read one of those Robert Frost poems she assigned."

"I sneaked a peek at 'The Road Not Taken' in science," Annie said. "It looks sort of interesting."

Daphne agreed. "Trying to find the cafeteria at lunch,

I felt like I could have written it. But I would have called it 'The Corridor Not Taken.' "

Annie and Jerry both laughed appreciatively. Daphne was pleased. Maybe this Jerry person was okay.

"And I like that teacher—Ms. McBain. Did you realize she never once talked about the difference between a colon and a semicolon?"

They were approaching the cafeteria entrance when Daphne heard her name again. She turned and waved at Kimmie, whose face was flushed with excitement.

"Have you seen my sister?" she asked breathlessly.

"No," Daphne said. "Kimmie, this is Jerry."

Kimmie's expression suddenly changed. She lowered her eyelids, giggled a little, and said, "Hi," in a funny sort of squeaky voice.

"What clubs are you going to join?" Annie asked.

A flash of concern crossed Kimmie's face. "I don't know! That's why I'm looking for my sister. She was supposed to tell me which ones to sign up for."

Jerry looked puzzled. "Can't you just sign up for the ones you're interested in?"

Kimmie seemed a bit shocked by that notion. "But I wouldn't know if they were the *right* ones! They might be full of nerds or something. I've gotta find Barbie." She hurried into the cafeteria.

"I don't get it," Jerry said.

"Her sister's just looking out for her," Daphne explained. "My sisters are like that, too. It's kind of nice, actually. They're just giving us advice so we don't do anything really stupid."

"Well, I don't have any older brothers or sisters," Jerry said cheerfully, "so I guess I'll just have to take my chances and run the risk of doing something stupid."

"C'mon," Annie said, "I want to go find the Creative Writing Club."

The three of them entered the cafeteria together. Daphne was amazed at how it had been transformed since the afternoon. Most of the tables had been moved out, and the ones that remained were rearranged in a circle around the rim of the room. A huge poster on one wall proclaimed "Get Involved!" And there were signs on each table identifying the various clubs and groups.

Behind the tables, representatives from the groups were busily talking to the kids gathered around. Daphne figured the representatives must be ninth graders. They had that look of being totally sure of themselves.

Annie seemed to read her thoughts. "Maybe after a couple of years of junior high we'll look like that."

Daphne nodded, but privately she was thinking she'd need more like ten years of junior high to develop that air of confidence.

The first table they passed was the Science Club. Daphne remembered what Barbie had said about it. But there was that nice girl from her science class signing up. What was her name?

"Hi, Barbara," she called softly.

The thin, dark-haired girl turned and grinned. "I have a pretty good idea you're not too interested in signing up here," she said.

Daphne acknowledged the fact with an abashed smile, and introduced her to Annie and Jerry.

"Any of you folks interested in science?" the older boy behind the table asked hopefully.

All three of them responded with head shakes that were both fervent and apologetic.

"Well, we can't all be nuclear physicists," Barbara said comfortingly. "Hey, any of you guys good in English?"

Annie, Jerry, and Daphne exchanged looks, responding with modest affirmatives.

"Great! I have the worst grammar in the universe. Let's make a deal—I'll help you guys in science, and you check my English papers for grammar, okay?"

"Sounds like a good deal to me," Annie said. The others agreed.

"She seems really nice," Annie remarked later as they moved on in search of the Creative Writing Club.

"I think so, too," Daphne said. She was amazed—only one day in junior high, and already she'd made two new friends, Jerry and Barbara. Actually, three, if she included Kimmie. Remembering Kimmie made her think again of what Barbie had said. Obviously, she was wrong about the Science Club. If there were kids like Barbara in it, the club couldn't be so nerdy.

The three were looking at some handouts the Drama Club was distributing when suddenly Daphne felt someone grab her.

"There you are!" A familiar voice cried out.

"Lydia!" Before she could say another word, her oldest sister started to pull her away.

"C'mon, there's something I want you to sign up for."

Daphne started to protest weakly, but her sister had that determined expression she knew all too well. "I'll meet you at the Creative Writing Club table," she called to Annie and Jerry, allowing herself to be dragged away.

"How was your first day?" Lydia asked.

"Pretty good," Daphne replied. "Where are you taking me?"

"I want you to sign up for a Student Council committee. There's a whole bunch of them. You can choose the one you like best."

"Gee, thanks," Daphne said, with just a touch of sarcasm in her voice. Lydia didn't seem to catch it, though.

"It's a good idea to get involved with the Student Council right from the start," Lydia explained. "That way you begin to build a power base."

What's a power base? Daphne wondered. But she didn't have time to ponder that. Along the way to the Student Council table, Lydia kept her busy meeting people, introducing her to so many kids she didn't have time to say much more than a brief "Nice to meet you."

"Gosh, you know everyone!" Daphne said admiringly. She had to admit it was nice being taken care of like this. She'd never meet so many people on her own! And she marveled at the way people seemed to automatically accept her, just because she was Lydia's sister.

"This is Rick Lewis," Lydia said, indicating a tall, handsome boy who stood behind the Student Council table. "He's president of the Student Council. Rick, this is my sister Daphne. She's just started the seventh grade."

The unconcealed pride in Lydia's voice made Daphne feel warm all over. The boy grinned at her, and Daphne felt herself go tingly. She smiled shyly.

"Hi, Daphne," Rick Lewis said. "Glad to meet you. What are you interested in?"

"Gee, I don't know." She looked at the list of committees. There was the Legislative Committee, the Course Evaluation Committee, the Canned Food Drive Committee, the Social Events Committee—none of them meant anything to her. She turned to Lydia helplessly.

"Maybe the Social Action Committee," Lydia murmured, looking over Daphne's shoulder at the list.

Rick Lewis looked at Daphne knowingly. "If you're Lydia's sister, I know what you're really interested in." He indicated a sheet of paper with the heading "Seventh Grade—Pres." Four names were scrawled under it.

"What's that?" Daphne asked.

"It's the names of people who want to run for president of the seventh grade. How about it?"

Daphne's mouth dropped open. She looked at her sister frantically.

"No, I don't think Daphne's up for that," Lydia said.

Waves of grateful relief washed over her.

"But what about vice-president?"

"Lydia!" Daphne gasped. Surely her sister was kidding.

Rick Lewis indicated another sheet. "Yeah, okay, there's only two people signed up."

Daphne felt positively sick. Here was this Rick Lewis, smiling at her in such an encouraging way. But vice-president of the seventh grade?

"Oh, come on," Lydia urged. "It'll be fun! I could be your campaign manager!"

"But I've never done anything like that, Lydia."

"Now, Daphne, just listen—" Lydia began, but she was interrupted.

"Daphne, I've been looking all over for you!" And for the second time that day, Cassie rescued her.

"Hey, Cass—what do you think of Daphne running for seventh-grade vice-president?" Lydia asked.

Cassie made a face. "Too much work. C'mon, I want to get you signed up for the Pep Club." She grabbed Daphne's arm.

Vaguely wondering if she was going to end the day with black-and-blue marks all over her arms, Daphne once again let herself be dragged away, flashing Lydia a look of apology—mingled with relief. Whatever the Pep Club was, it couldn't be as unappealing as the idea of running for class office.

"What does the Pep Club do?" she asked.

Her sister waved a hand in the air. "Oh, you know, school spirit stuff." Daphne wasn't sure what that meant, but she followed Cassie obediently.

"This is my little sister Daphne," Cassie announced to the two girls standing behind the Pep Club table. "Daphne, this is Amy and this is Sue. They're co-captains of the cheerleading squad!"

From the way Cassie spoke, Daphne had a funny

feeling she was supposed to curtsy or something. "That's nice," she said uncertainly. "Uh, what does the Pep Club do?"

Amy and Sue went into a rhapsodic description of pep rallies and parties and football games.

"We make all the posters," one of them—was it Amy?—said.

"And we're in charge of decorations for the Junior Princess pageant, plus all the publicity," Sue-maybe-Amy chimed in.

"Speaking of which, did you hear about Nancy Eckhart?" Cassie asked excitedly.

"No, what?" Sue-and-Amy responded in unison.

"Well, Claire said that Helen said that—"

Daphne lost track of the *saids* and looked around to see if she could spot Annie and Jerry and the Creative Writing Club. The crowd was starting to thin out. The lights blinked a couple of times.

"Closing time," the Amy-Sue people chimed, and started gathering up their handouts.

"Oh, no!" Daphne said in dismay. "I wanted to sign up for the Creative Writing Club."

Cassie wrinkled her nose. "Really, I don't think you want to do that, Daphne. I kind of think maybe they're nerds."

Lydia dashed up to them. "Hey, tell Mom I'll be home in time for dinner, okay? I've got to stay for the newspaper staff meeting." She started to run off, but turned and called to Daphne over her shoulder. "I've got a surprise for you! I'll tell you later!"

Her mind still on the Creative Writing Club, Daphne only nodded. The one club she'd really wanted to join—and now it might be too late. Would they let her join tomorrow? It wasn't until later, walking home with Cassie and half-listening to her sister's chatter about how much fun the Pep Club would be, that Daphne wondered what Lydia's surprise could be.

She found out at dinner.

Everyone was talking at the same time. Mrs. Gray was giving a vivid description of her first day teaching English at the high school.

"It's the oddest feeling standing there in front of the class with all those eyes on you, soaking up everything you say. Of course, there were a few who didn't seem to be listening at all. There was one girl who kept pulling out a little mirror and fiddling with her hair." She frowned and looked at Cassie. "I hope none of you behave like that in your classes."

Cassie's head jerked up. "Who, me?" she asked innocently.

Daphne suppressed a giggle. She had a pretty good suspicion that the little mirror Cassie carried everywhere had been pulled out more than once that day.

"I had a super day," Fee said happily. "I got my hall monitor badge and I caught two third graders stepping out of line on the way to lunch."

"What did they get for that?" Mr. Gray asked. "Hard labor or life imprisonment?"

"Well, it was the first day, so I thought I'd show them a little mercy. But I told them if I caught them doing

45

it again, they'd be in *big* trouble. You gotta know how to handle these troublemakers."

Mr. Gray nodded seriously and turned to his wife. "I think our youngest daughter may have a future as a benevolent dictator. I wonder if she can make a living at it?"

Mrs. Gray laughed. "How was your day, Daphne?" she asked.

"It was good! I like most of my classes, and I met some new kids, and—"

Cassie jumped in. "She's signed up for the Pep Club."

"And the Student Council," Lydia added. She grinned at Daphne. "I put your name down."

"Which committee did you sign me up for?"

Lydia's eyes sparkled. "No committee. I put you down to run for seventh-grade vice-president."

Daphne stared at her sister. Her stomach started to churn and she could actually feel her heart thumping.

"It'll be great fun," Lydia said enthusiastically. She turned to her mother. "I'll be her campaign manager."

Daphne felt her father looking at her curiously. "I didn't know you were interested in that kind of thing. Do you *want* to be seventh-grade vice-president?"

Daphne didn't want to say. It certainly wasn't anything she'd ever considered. But Lydia was looking so pleased with herself and so proud of her that Daphne decided her sister was only doing what she thought was best for her. She must be right.

"I guess so," she said.

"It's a great way to meet lots of people," Lydia said.

Her mother was smiling, too. "I'm surprised! I never thought of you as the political type. But this could be a wonderful brand-new experience."

Daphne nodded. It would definitely be a brand-new experience. As for wonderful, she wasn't sure. But since Lydia looked so happy, Daphne tried very hard to look happy, too.

5

THANK YOU FOR THE RIDE, Mrs. Gray," Annie said politely as they pulled up in front of the school.

"Thanks, Mom," Lydia, Cassie, and Daphne echoed.

"You're welcome, girls," Mrs. Gray replied. "Service is cheerfully provided on rainy days. Sprinkles don't count, though—it has to be pouring."

And it was. Cassie looked out the window. "My hair's going to frizz," she wailed.

"Just run between the drops," Lydia advised, opening her door and jumping out.

"Lydia, where's your umbrella?" their mother yelled after her. But Lydia was already halfway to the school door.

Cassie was still looking mournfully out of the window. "Maybe it will stop in a minute."

"Cassie—go!" Mrs. Gray ordered. "I don't want to be late for school!"

Taking a deep breath, Cassie opened the back door slightly and thrust out her umbrella. Opening it, she then tried to maneuver herself out of the car and under the umbrella before a single drop could touch her.

Daphne and Annie followed, clutching their umbrellas tightly. Despite their efforts, with the rain coming from all directions they were showing the effects of the downpour by the time they got into the entrance hallway.

Cassie was fingering her hair. "Look at me," she moaned. "It's a good thing we're early. What if somebody saw me like this?"

The hallway was practically deserted. Mrs. Gray had to be at her school a full half hour before the girls had to be at theirs.

"Anyone want to come with me to the audiovisual room?" Cassie asked.

Lydia looked puzzled. "What do you want to go there for?"

Cassie opened her pocketbook to reveal a small blow dryer tucked inside. "It's the only place I can plug this in."

Daphne touched her own hair. It was just a little damp. And Annie's hair was naturally frizzy—a little rain hadn't made any difference.

Lydia ran her fingers through her closely cropped

hair. "Mine's almost dry. Hey, Daphne—I don't have any meetings after school today. We can start planning your Student Council campaign."

"Not today," Cassie stated flatly. "There's the first big Pep Club meeting and she has to come to that. I'd better go get started on my hair." She headed down the hall toward the girls' bathroom, her wet shoes making a squishy sound in the empty hallway.

"Okay," Lydia said. "Tonight, then. See ya." And she took off.

Daphne stared after them. Funny how they'd both been talking to her—but she hadn't said a thing.

Annie was looking at her in surprise. "What was all that about a Student Council campaign?"

"I'm running for seventh-grade vice-president."

Annie's mouth dropped open. "You're kidding! . . . Not that you wouldn't be good at anything you want to do," she added hastily, "but do you really want to do that?"

"Sure," Daphne said, hoping she sounded more confident than she felt. "Lydia says it's a lot of fun."

"What about this Pep Club? What do they do?"

"I'm not absolutely sure. But Cassie says it's the most important club at school. Maybe you should join it, too."

Annie shook her head. "I'm going to be busy with the Creative Writing Club. Aren't you going to join?"

Daphne sighed. Could she possibly have time to belong to two clubs and run for class office? When would she have time for homework? But she couldn't imagine her and Annie not doing the same thing.

Annie's voice dropped to a whisper. "Look—there's Mr. Hudson."

Daphne turned and saw their handsome homeroom teacher coming from the main office. He was examining a sheet of paper and frowning slightly. When he saw the girls, his expression changed.

"Hi! You kids get caught in the rain?"

"Yeah, a little bit," Annie said, her face turning red. Daphne studied his shoes.

"I just picked up the list of students who signed up for the Drama Club. I'm the faculty advisor." He glanced at the list and shook his head. "It doesn't look like there are too many budding actors in this class. Either of you two interested?"

Even in her worst nightmares, Daphne couldn't picture herself standing on a stage in front of an audience.

"Not me," Annie said. "I don't have any talent. And Daphne'd never go on stage. She's shy."

Daphne looked sorrowfully at her friend. Annie was right, of course—but did she have to tell the world?

"I understand," Mr. Hudson said pleasantly. "Well, there's always backstage work, painting scenery, that sort of thing. Maybe you two might be interested in that."

"Maybe," Annie allowed. "I joined the Creative Writing Club."

"That's a good group," Mr. Hudson said. "How about you?"

Daphne bit her lower lip. "I wanted to join it, too, but I didn't get to it yesterday."

"Maybe you can sign up today," Mr. Hudson suggested. "I've got to run. I'll see you girls in class."

More students were starting to come into the building, and Daphne tugged Annie aside. "Annie," she murmured pleadingly, "you shouldn't tell people I'm shy." Who would ever elect a shy person to class office?

But Annie misunderstood. "Yeah, I guess people can figure it out for themselves."

Later, Mr. Hudson had just finished taking roll in homeroom when the bells rang for the morning announcements.

"The following clubs will have organizational meetings immediately following the last class," a voice came over the intercom. "The Science Club, in room 234; the Math Club, in 253; the Creative Writing Club, in 309; and the Pep Club, in the gym.

The Student Council is pleased to announce the candidates for seventh-grade office. Running for president are Laura Abrams, David Bailey, Mark Lindsay, and Judy Stevenson. The candidates for vice-president are Eliot Carson, Nancy Findlay, and Daphne Gray."

Daphne had been waiting apprehensively for the sound of her own name blared throughout the school on the loudspeaker. When it came, she could feel her face getting hot, and she didn't even remember the names of the candidates for the rest of the offices.

Luckily, few kids noticed her reaction—they hadn't learned everyone's name yet. Only the two kids she knew from Eastside, Carol and Bobby, turned to her with puzzled expressions.

Someone else was looking at her curiously, too. And when the bell rang, Mr. Hudson spoke to her on her way to the door.

"So you're running for class vice-president," he said, smiling. "I thought you were supposed to be so shy!"

Now he probably thought she and Annie were lying, Daphne thought miserably. She nodded uncertainly. "It's actually my sister's idea. She likes that political stuff."

His eyebrows shot up. "Is your sister Lydia Gray?"

Daphne nodded again.

"Well, well," he mused. "I never would have guessed you were Lydia's sister. You have another sister here at school, too, don't you?"

"Cassie."

"I don't know her," Mr. Hudson said. "It must be nice having two sisters looking out for you."

How many more times would she hear that this week? Daphne wondered. She was so tired of it! Then, aware of what she was feeling, she pushed the disloyal thoughts from her mind.

"Yes, it's very nice," she said quickly.

At least she'd always have people to eat lunch with. As she strolled into the cafeteria, she had to admit it felt good to see Cassie waving to her. Barbie, Kimmie, and another vaguely familiar-looking girl were sitting there, too. Making her way to the table, Daphne saw Annie walking in the opposite direction. She was surprised to see her friend carrying a lunch bag. Hadn't

Annie heard what Cassie had said yesterday about lunch bags?

"Annie, we're over here," she called, pointing to the table where her sister and the others were sitting.

"Oh. I was thinking maybe we could sit with Jerry and those kids over there."

Daphne looked in the direction Annie was indicating. She could see Jerry and three kids she recognized from their English class. She wondered what they were talking about.

"Daphne!"

Cassie was calling to her. Daphne turned to Annie with a look of resignation. "I guess I'd better go sit with Cassie. Are you sure you can't eat with us?" She could hear the faint note of pleading in her own voice.

Annie must have heard it, too. She sighed. "Well, okay. But tomorrow let's sit with Jerry, okay?"

Cassie had saved seats for them.

"Annie, this is Alison," she said, introducing the familiar-looking girl. "She's head of the Pep Club Publicity Committee. Did you sign up for the Pep Club yesterday?"

Annie shook her head, and Cassie frowned. "You really should, Annie. Everyone belongs to the Pep Club." She turned to Daphne. "We're trying to decide which committee we should put you guys on."

"Kimmie should be on the school spirit squad," Alison said. "Kimmie, you're so perky and all you'd be great at getting kids to show up for games."

Kimmie responded with an appropriately perky grin. "That sounds neat," she said happily.

"What about you, Daphne?" Alison asked.

Daphne shifted in her seat. No one had ever called *her* perky. "Do I have to be on a committee?"

"Of course you do," Cassie said firmly. "Everyone's on a committee. We just want you to get on a good one. Oh—and you, too, Annie."

Annie paused between bites of her sandwich. "I told you, I didn't sign up yesterday."

"Well, you can still join," Barbie informed her. "Just come to the meeting this afternoon."

"Can't," Annie replied. "I've got a Creative Writing Club meeting."

"Oh." Barbie turned away in a manner that suggested Annie no longer held any interest for them. "Now, girls," she said, her eyes shifting back and forth between Daphne and Kimmie, "you have to remember that as seventh graders, you're at the bottom level in the Pep Club. So you can't expect to get any really top-notch assignments—like liaison with the football team, that sort of thing."

"That's okay," Daphne said fervently.

"But you can work your way up," Cassie said brightly. "I mean, this year you might get stuck with refreshments, or decorations. But if you do a really good job and don't complain, everyone will respect you and next year—who knows?—you might even get on the Junior Princess Committee!"

Alison and Barbie confirmed this with vigorous nods.

"Gee," Kimmie said, her eyes shining. "I just love junior high! It's so exciting!" Her smile faded a bit. "Except for the classes. Boy, they really pile on the homework." She turned to Daphne. "In my English class, we have to read poems! Can you believe that? Double yuck."

Daphne caught Annie's expression. Her friend's lips were quivering from holding in a laugh and she was rolling her eyes.

"Have you girls met any boys yet?" Barbie asked.

"Boys?" Daphne echoed.

"*Boys,*" Barbie repeated. "You know, like guys."

What was she getting at? Daphne thought of Jerry. "Well, sure, I met a boy in my English class."

Kimmie gave her an admiring look. "Wow, I haven't met any really cute guys yet."

Cassie beamed proudly at her sister. "Fast work, Daphne! Tell us about him!"

Daphne looked at her in bewilderment. "He's just a boy. I mean, he's nice and all, but I don't know him very well yet. I guess we'll be friends. . . ."

"Go for it!" Cassie exclaimed. "If you can get a boyfriend right at the beginning of the term, you're set for all the dances and for the football games over at the high school."

A boyfriend? Jerry? She looked at Annie for help, but her friend just shrugged.

Barbie made a dismissive gesture. "You shouldn't waste any time on seventh-grade boys. They're so immature."

Alison bobbed her head in agreement. "You'll meet some eighth-grade boys in the Pep Club," Alison assured them. "You won't believe how much boys can mature in one year."

"Eighth-grade boys," Kimmie murmured in awe. "Wow."

"I met a ninth-grade boy at the Extracurricular Fair yesterday," Daphne offered. "His name was Rick Lewis."

"Rick Lewis!" Alison, Barbie, and Cassie repeated the name in unison.

Barbie sighed. "Now that's what I call a major hunk."

"Don't even think about Rick Lewis," Alison advised. "Seventh-grade girls don't go with ninth-grade boys."

Daphne couldn't imagine someone like Rick Lewis paying attention to her anyway. But she was curious. "Why not?"

"They get bad reputations," Cassie said. "You're supposed to go with guys just one year older." She paused, and turned to Barbie. "But you know, I don't think it's a bad idea for her to go with that seventh grader she was talking about. What's his name?"

"Jerry."

"Maybe you could get some practice with this Jerry."

Daphne was puzzled. "Practice doing what?"

"Flirting!" Cassie exclaimed. "You could start with Jerry."

Barbie contemplated this. "Maybe that's not a bad idea. As long as you don't stay with him too long."

"Okay, you've got Daphne fixed up," Kimmie said. "Now what about me?"

Barbie patted her arm. "Don't worry. We'll find someone for you."

"And you too, Annie," Cassie added.

Annie suddenly stood up. "I've gotta get to class."

Daphne looked at the clock. "We've got fifteen minutes!"

"I want to go over my homework," Annie murmured. Grabbing her books, she left the table without even saying good-bye.

What was the matter with her? Daphne wondered, looking after Annie's retreating figure.

Cassie, Barbie, and Alison were having a whispered conference.

"Daphne," Cassie said suddenly. "Take off your glasses."

Startled, Daphne obeyed. Cassie looked at Barbie and Alison, and they all nodded.

"Much better," Barbie said. "You've got pretty eyes."

"Glasses make people look like brains," Alison added. "They give the wrong impression."

"Why don't you get contacts?" Kimmie asked. "I've got them. Look."

Daphne could barely make out Kimmie's eyes, let alone the contact lenses in them. "I've never wanted contacts," she admitted. "When I think of sticking something in my eyes, it makes me feel sick."

"Can't you manage without your glasses?" Barbie asked.

"I wouldn't be able to see the board in class," Daphne replied.

"Well, you can wear them in class," Cassie said, "but take them off the minute the bell rings. You pretty much know your way around the building now, don't you? I mean, you don't really have to be able to see."

Later on, Daphne gave it a try. She found she could actually make it all the way to English class without her glasses. Of course, when a couple of people said hi to her in the halls, she had no idea who they were.

The minute she got into class, she put them back on. Annie was in her seat. Daphne tried to catch her friend's eye, but Annie was staring straight ahead. Jerry saw her, though, and waved.

She barely heard Ms. McBain's opening remarks to the class. She was thinking about what Cassie had said. Would she want Jerry to be her boyfriend? She sneaked a peek. He was kind of cute and seemed nice . . . and if Cassie thought it was really important to have a boyfriend . . .

"Daphne?"

All thoughts of boyfriends rushed from her head. Ms. McBain was frowning at her.

"Are you all right, Daphne? This is the second time I've called your name."

Daphne could feel her cheeks burning. "Uh, I'm sorry, Ms. McBain. I guess I was daydreaming."

Ms. McBain's frown faded, but she still looked serious. "Well, this isn't the place for it. We were discussing 'The Road Not Taken,' by Robert Frost. What do you think this poem is really about?"

Daphne thought frantically, hoping to get back in Ms. McBain's good graces. Thank goodness she'd read the poem several times. "I think," she said carefully, "it's about making choices. And how you never know if the choice you make is the right one."

"And for that reason, making choices is never easy, is it?" Ms. McBain said.

Daphne nodded.

Annie raised her hand. "Sometimes making choices is so hard you let other people make them for you."

Ms. McBain considered this. "True, but I don't think that's what the poet is saying."

Daphne turned and looked at Annie. But her best friend was still staring straight ahead.

When class was finished, Jerry came over to her.

"Are you coming to the Creative Writing Club meeting this afternoon, Daphne?" he asked.

Was he flirting with her? Daphne wondered. Did he especially want her to come?

"I didn't get to sign up yesterday," she told him.

"You can still join," Jerry said. "You can come to the meeting and sign up there."

Annie joined them. "What's up?" she asked.

Daphne looked at her. Her tone was casual enough, but something was wrong. Daphne always knew when something was bothering Annie. But she couldn't always tell what the problem was.

"Jerry said I could come to the Creative Writing Club meeting this afternoon and sign up there."

"But didn't Cassie say you have to go to the Pep Club meeting?"

"Maybe I could get out of it," Daphne suggested.

"Suit yourself," Annie said, and walked out.

Daphne watched her go. What was the matter with Annie? Was she angry at her? For what?

She forgot all about flirting with Jerry. "Uh, maybe I'll be there," she told him, hurrying out.

She really did want to join the club. Then she could

see Annie and find out what was wrong. Cassie would be furious, though, if she missed the Pep Club meeting. But maybe she could find her first and explain, and let Cassie put her on any committee she liked—maybe she'd understand.

For the rest of the day, she hoped she'd run into Cassie between classes, but she didn't see her anywhere. At one point, Daphne thought she saw Barbie, and she debated whether to simply give Barbie a message to pass on to Cassie. No, she decided, that wouldn't do at all. She owed it to Cassie to give her an in-person explanation. After all, her sister was trying so hard to help her. . . .

She was surprised and pleased to find Jerry waiting for her after the last class.

"Annie told me this was your last class," he said. "She's supposed to meet us here to go to the Creative Writing Club meeting."

"I have to go find my sister first," Daphne said.

"Okay. We'll meet you in the room."

On the way to the gym, Daphne realized she was still wearing her glasses. Quickly, she took them off. She stood at the gym entrance, watching kids stream in. Without her glasses, they all looked like a blur. But she managed to recognize Cassie's bright blue shirtdress approaching.

"Cassie," she said, approaching her rapidly. "Listen, I wanted to tell you—"

But she got no further.

"Daphne, this is Melissa Morgan," Cassie said, her

tone suggesting she was introducing the Queen of England. "Melissa is president of the Pep Club."

"Hi, Daphne," Melissa said. "Cassie's been telling me all about you."

"Pleased to meet you," Daphne said politely. "Cassie, listen, I—"

But again, Cassie wouldn't let her finish. "Daphne really wants to get involved in the Pep Club, Melissa. Isn't that great! It feels so neat having my little sister following me!"

She was looking at Daphne with an expression that had never been bestowed on her before, at least not by Cassie—a mixture of enthusiasm, affection, and real honest-to-goodness pride.

Daphne's heart sunk. How could she possibly let her sister down?

"Let's go," Melissa said. "It wouldn't do for the president to be late for her own club meeting!"

As she followed them into the gym, Daphne suddenly had the oddest image of herself. She was like a robot, programmed to do what she was supposed to do.

And not what *she* wanted.

6

ANNIE WASN'T WAITING FOR HER in the usual place the next morning. Daphne stayed as long as she dared, until she was afraid she'd be late for homeroom.

By the time she raced into the room, there was no time to talk. The bell rang just as she took her seat. Annie was there in her usual seat right next to her, but didn't even greet her.

Mr. Hudson looked a little harried. "Kids, I have to run out to my car and get some books I left there. I'd tell you to sit quietly and study, but I'm not that naive. So if you don't mind, just keep your conversations down to a dull roar and I'll be right back."

The minute he left the room, everyone started talking. Daphne immediately turned to Annie.

"What's the matter?"

Annie seemed reluctant to face her. "Nothing."

"C'mon, Annie! I know when something's bugging you!"

Annie finally turned and faced her. "Do you like Jerry?"

"Well, sure," Daphne replied. "He's really nice."

"I mean, do you *like* him?" Annie persisted.

Now Daphne was thoroughly confused. "Annie, what are you talking about?"

Annie looked distinctly uncomfortable. "Well, the way you and Cassie were talking about him yesterday, about Jerry being a possible boyfriend and all that . . ."

Daphne looked at her blankly. Then something clicked. "Annie! You like Jerry! I mean, you *like* him!"

Annie's freckles blended together into a blush. "This is embarrassing," she mumbled. "I sound like that dippy Kimmie."

Daphne shook her head vigorously. "No, you don't! C'mon, am I right? Do you like him?"

Annie's blush deepened. She grinned, rolled her eyes, and shrugged. Finally, she nodded.

"That's neat!" Daphne exclaimed. "Why didn't you tell me?"

"I was going to, yesterday. Then when you started talking about him at lunch, how you were going to start flirting with him and all that—"

"I didn't say that," Daphne objected. "That was Cassie's idea."

"Well, you were going along with it."

Was she? She couldn't remember saying much of anything.

"Look, Annie, if you like Jerry, I think that's great! And I won't flirt with him, I promise. I probably wouldn't know how, anyway."

Finally, Annie smiled. "Okay."

Daphne sighed in relief. She couldn't bear to have Annie angry with her. And she'd never even thought about Jerry in that way until Cassie had brought it up.

"Do you think Jerry likes you? I mean, I know he likes you, but does he *like* you?"

"I don't know for sure," Annie replied, "but I think maybe. He said he might come over this weekend."

"Wow," Daphne said. So Annie would have a boyfriend. For some reason, she thought of Rick Lewis, that cute boy Lydia had introduced her to—the president of the Student Council. Of course, that was just a fantasy.

Annie interrupted her daydream. "Daphne, are you sure you don't like Jerry, too? I mean, I know you like him, but do you *like* him?"

Daphne shook her head. "Not that way. If he's going to be your boyfriend, he'll be my friend, but that's all."

Annie looked at her skeptically. "Well, you were thinking about something or somebody just now. You had the funniest expression."

Daphne blushed slightly and lowered her voice. "I was sort of thinking about somebody," she admitted. Then she told Annie about meeting Rick Lewis.

Annie was impressed. "A ninth grader!"

"Oh, I don't think he could ever be interested in me," Daphne said quickly. "Cassie says seventh-grade girls never go with ninth-gráde boys. Besides, he's president of the Student Council! He probably likes girls like Lydia—you know, girls who do political things."

"You're doing something political," Annie pointed out. "You're running for seventh-grade vice-president."

Daphne had almost forgotten about that. "Oh, yeah," she murmured, "that's right."

Annie's expression was curious. "You don't look too thrilled about it."

She wasn't. Every time she thought about it, she felt queasy.

"Lydia says—" she began, but Annie interrupted her.

"Do you have to do everything Lydia says?" Annie asked.

"No, of course not! But . . ." Suddenly Daphne wanted very much to change the subject. "How was the Creative Writing Club meeting?"

"It was super," Annie said. "We talked about what we like to write and what we want to try writing. And we talked about how we get ideas, that sort of thing."

Daphne was full of envy. Those were the kinds of things she and Annie always talked about. And now Annie was talking about them with other people.

"Ms. McBain's the advisor," Annie continued, "and she says maybe we can start a literary magazine for the school. Then we could publish our own poems and stories."

"Wow," Daphne breathed. To see her own poems in

print! Of course, she'd probably just sign them *Anonymous*. And then her heart sank. When would she have time to write any poems?

"Oh, Daphne, you should have been there. I think you can still join, though."

"I wish I could," Daphne said. "But—" She was about to say "Lydia says," then thought better of it. "If I'm running for class office, I don't think I'll have time for another club," she lamented.

She paused. "Maybe . . . maybe I could just be on a Student Council committee instead of running for class officer."

"That sounds like a good idea," Annie said encouragingly.

The more Daphne thought about it, the better it sounded. Lydia wouldn't be too happy about it, but as long as she was on a committee, maybe her sister wouldn't be too disappointed.

"Did you end up going to the Pep Club meeting yesterday?"

"Yeah, I had to. Cassie was so excited about it. And there were all these other kids around. I just couldn't tell her I didn't want to go. She would have been furious."

"What was it like?"

Daphne made a face. "I thought it was all kind of silly. This girl, Melissa, made a speech about how important school spirit is, and how kids have to be loyal to their school. And there was this big argument about what kind of T-shirts they're going to have made."

"What were they arguing about?"

Daphne sighed. "Some kids wanted red shirts with white letters. Others wanted white shirts with red letters."

"You're kidding! That's what they were making a big fuss about?"

Daphne sighed and nodded. "And now Cassie's got me on the Promotion Committee. I'm supposed to write these announcements to get kids to come to the football games." She grinned ruefully. "Cassie says I should write little poems and they'll pass them around the school. But how can I write poems about football games? I've never even been to one!"

"What else happened?"

Daphne sighed again. It seemed like she'd been doing that a lot lately. "Someone brought up the idea of starting a dating service."

"A *what*?"

"A dating service. Boys and girls would fill out forms describing themselves, and then the Pep Club would match them up for a dance."

Annie's response was immediate. "Gross."

Daphne couldn't argue with her. "Kimmie thinks it's a wonderful idea."

"She would."

Daphne couldn't resist a giggle. "She *is* kind of dippy, isn't she?"

"No kidding," Annie said. "Why do we always have to eat lunch with her?"

"Well, she's Barbie's sister, and Barbie's Cassie's best

friend, and Cassie thinks Kimmie and I should be friends, too."

Annie rolled her eyes. "Well, that doesn't mean I have to be her friend."

But they'd always had the same friends, Daphne thought.

Just then Mr. Hudson returned carrying a stack of books, and everyone got quiet. He took roll. Just as he finished, the intercom bells chimed.

"Good morning," the voice crackled. "May I have your attention for the morning announcements? Students wishing to sign up for the field trip to the Chicago Planetarium must bring consent forms to the office by Friday. The Explorers Club will meet this afternoon in room 312. If they can find it. Ha-ha."

The announcer had a weird sense of humor, Daphne thought, only half-listening. But the next announcement made her sit up straight.

"Congratulations to the newly selected editor of the *Cedar Century*, George Philips."

Oh no, thought Daphne. Poor Lydia!

"The judges are probably sexist," Annie whispered to her.

Either that, Daphne decided, or they were afraid Lydia would rouse the students to total revolution. Her heart swelled with sympathy for her sister.

When the bell rang, she and Annie moved toward the door together.

"I guess Lydia will be really disappointed," Annie said.

Daphne nodded. "She was so sure she'd be the new editor. It meant a lot to her."

"Oh, well—she'll just find something else to get excited about," Annie said philosophically.

Daphne agreed. "She always does."

They separated and Daphne headed for her science class. She was just about to go into the room when something on the opposite wall in the hallway caught her eye.

"The best man for the job! Eliot Carson for 7th Grade Vice-President!" read the sign.

Daphne stared at it, trying to envision her own name on a sign. The image wasn't very appealing. What did vice-presidents do, anyway?

"I think that's supposed to be a joke," came a voice from behind her. Daphne turned and saw Rick Lewis standing there.

"What do you mean?" she asked nervously. She realized she'd forgotten to take off her glasses when she left homeroom. Would she look too stupid if she took them off right now?

Rick indicated the sign. "He's the *only* boy running for vice-president."

"Oh." Daphne touched her glasses self-consciously. "I didn't realize people would be putting up signs so soon."

"Oh, sure," Rick said. "By tomorrow the walls will be plastered." He grinned. "But don't worry—if Lydia's running your campaign, your signs will be bigger than anyone's."

Daphne was feeling queasy again. She wasn't sure if it was the thought of the campaign or the sight of Rick Lewis. Actually, she was kind of glad she'd kept her glasses on—he was so cute.

"Lydia's a real politician," Rick added.

"I know," Daphne said. "I've never been the political type."

He seemed surprised. "Oh, yeah? Then how come you're running?"

Daphne didn't want to admit it was all Lydia's idea. "I thought it might be fun," she said lamely. She looked at the sign again. "Now I'm not so sure."

"You can always drop out," Rick said cheerfully. "And if you do, we could sure use you on the Social Action Committee." He glanced up at the clock. "I've gotta run. See ya later."

Daphne drifted into class in a daze. He was so nice! And he actually seemed interested in her! And if she dropped out of the election, maybe she could be on his committee. . . .

But all thoughts of Rick Lewis flew out of her head with the teacher's opening words to the class.

"Close all books and take out a piece of paper and a pencil. We're having a pop quiz on today's assignment."

Daphne stared at him aghast as he drew a blobby-looking thing on the blackboard.

"You will identify this and name each part," he instructed.

She looked at the diagram dismally. It could have been graffiti as far as she was concerned. She had read the assignment, but not all that carefully. And those awful names—they didn't mean anything! How could she remember words like *amoeba* and *molecule* and *proto-something?*

Later as they were passing the papers forward, her friend in the next seat turned to her. "How'd you do?"

"Awful," Daphne groaned. "Barbara, I just don't get this stuff."

"It's really not that hard," Barbara said. "You just have to organize it so it all makes sense."

"How?"

The teacher had started talking, so Barbara just whispered, "After class."

When the bell rang, Daphne turned to Barbara eagerly. "Do you think you could help me?"

"Sure," Barbara said. "We can get together and go over this stuff."

"When?"

"How about tonight, after dinner?"

"Great," Daphne said. "Do you want to come over to my house or should I come to yours?"

"I'd better come to your house," Barbara said. "I've got two little brothers and it's noisy around my place."

"With three sisters, it's not much more quiet around mine," Daphne noted glumly, writing down her address. She was still thinking about the quiz. She'd never flunked a test in her life.

Oh, well, she thought philosophically a few minutes later as she headed toward the gym—it's just one quiz. She knew there'd be more. Lost in thought as she started downstairs to the girls' locker room, she almost bumped smack into Lydia.

"Oh, Lydia," she said, "I'm so sorry!"

Her sister didn't look particularly depressed. But she was definitely angry.

"I can't believe they picked George," she sniffed. "He's such a wimp! He wants to put a dumb gossip column in the paper! And he's afraid of anything that's the least bit controversial." She shook her head grimly. "Now I'm not even sure if I want to stay on the staff."

"Really? But if you stay on the staff, you might have some influence on him. Besides, you love working on the paper."

"I'm not going to love taking orders from that jerk." And then Lydia brightened. "Anyway, if I drop off the *Century* staff, I'll have more time to devote to your campaign! That'll cheer me up. I love a good political battle!"

This was definitely not the time to tell her sister she didn't want to run, Daphne decided. "Great," she said, only hoping her smile wasn't too thin.

Now she wasn't just a candidate, she thought later on as she attacked the parallel bars with a vengeance. She was a serious candidate. And with Lydia giving her undivided attention to the campaign, Daphne suddenly realized she might actually win.

Daphne Gray—seventh-grade vice-president. She lost her grip, fell on her rear, and didn't even feel it.

Later on she confided her despair to Annie as they walked into the cafeteria together. "She's so disappointed about not being editor. If I told her I didn't want to be vice-president, she'd feel even worse! I just can't do that to her. And on top of everything else, I think I flunked my science pop quiz this morning."

Annie groaned. "I'm having an awful time in science, too. It just doesn't make any sense."

Daphne had an inspiration. "That nice girl in my class, Barbara, is coming over after dinner tonight to help me. Why don't you come, too?"

"Great, I will," Annie said, turning to wave to Jerry, who was sitting at a table with a couple of kids from their English class. "Let's go sit with them," she urged.

Daphne glanced surreptitiously at the table where Cassie and a bunch of Pep Club people were eating. Her sister was absorbed in a conversation and hadn't noticed her yet.

Suddenly Daphne didn't think she could handle one more conversation devoted to the Pep Club or spend one more lunch listening to Kimmie giggle.

"Okay," she agreed. But even as she accompanied Annie to the table, she couldn't help feeling just a little bit disloyal.

The kids at the table were talking about the Creative Writing Club.

"I think the magazine should be strictly for poetry," one girl said.

Jerry disagreed. "If it's just poetry, we won't get a big audience. I think there should be stories, too."

"And art," Annie chimed in. "Drawings, and maybe photographs."

Everyone started talking at once. Daphne couldn't

really join in—after all, she wasn't even a member of the club. But it was fun just listening.

Suddenly she was aware of someone standing by her side. She looked up and practically winced at Cassie's glare.

"I didn't even see you come in!"

Daphne couldn't think of any answer, so she just smiled weakly and shrugged.

"Kimmie's got something important to tell you," Cassie continued.

What could Kimmie possibly have to tell her? "Excuse me for a sec," she murmured to the others at the table. Then she followed Cassie back to where her sister was sitting.

"Take off your glasses," Cassie whispered.

Reluctantly, Daphne did. She could barely make out Kimmie's face, but could tell she was excited.

"I'm having a party this Friday!"

"Is it your birthday?" Daphne asked.

"No, silly, not that kind of party. A real party, with dancing! And boys! Just seventh-grade boys, of course. But like Barbie says, we need practice! Can you come?"

"Of course she can," Cassie replied happily.

It didn't sound very appealing. But what could she say? Cassie was already annoyed with her for not sitting with them. She didn't want to make her any angrier.

"I guess so," she said. Then a thought occurred to her. "Can my friend Annie come too?"

Kimmie didn't look too thrilled with the idea. "I've already got an even number of boys and girls."

"But Annie's my best friend," Daphne said. Surely

even someone as dippy as Kimmie could understand what that meant.

"That doesn't mean you have to do everything together," Cassie suggested.

"She might not fit in," Kimmie said.

Daphne looked at her in bewilderment. How could *she* fit in and not Annie? "What's that supposed to mean?" she demanded.

Kimmie sort of squirmed in her seat. "No offense, Daphne, but she's not exactly cool, if you know what I mean."

Daphne felt herself getting angry. "*I* think she's cool."

Kimmie didn't even seem to hear her. "I only want certain people. You know, the right kind. Not just anybody."

"Annie's not just anybody! And if you don't want her to come, I don't think I want to come either."

"Daphne!" Cassie exclaimed.

Kimmie sort of squirmed in her seat. "Well, I guess it would be okay. . . ."

Daphne looked back longingly at the table she had left. "Is that all you had to tell me?"

Kimmie nodded.

"I'd better get back to my friends," Daphne said. Even with her back to them, she could feel Cassie's disapproving eyes.

7

I DON'T THINK QUITTING the newspaper staff is such a good idea," Mr. Gray remarked to Lydia as they were all finishing dessert. "It sounds like sour grapes to me."

Lydia scowled. "It's just not going to be any fun with that jerk for an editor. Besides, this way I'll have more time to help Daphne with her campaign for vice-president."

"Lydia," Daphne asked, "what does the Social Action Committee do?"

"Different things," her sister replied. "They run the canned food drive at Thanksgiving to collect food for poor people. And they sponsor a foster child in South America. Oh, and last year, when this boy at school was in a terrible accident, they raised money for an operation. Why do you want to know?"

Daphne took a deep breath. "I was talking to Rick Lewis today—"

"Who's Rick Lewis?" Phoebe interrupted.

"He's in the ninth grade," Lydia said, "and he's president of the Student Council."

"And he's cute," Cassie added. "But remember what I told you about seventh-grade girls and ninth-grade boys. You could get a reputation."

"That's silly," Lydia stated. "Rick Lewis is one of the nicest guys I know. If Daphne likes him, I think it's perfectly okay."

"This could be very embarrassing," Cassie said. "My seventh-grade sister with a ninth grader! I don't even have a boyfriend—yet," she added quickly.

Daphne couldn't believe this. "I just said I was talking to him! He's not my boyfriend." *Yet,* a little voice inside her whispered. She pushed the thought away quickly. How could she even dream about it? "Anyway, he said they could use me on the Social Action Committee."

"You can't be on a committee *and* be a class officer," Lydia objected. "It's against the rules."

"I might not win the election," Daphne said.

"You'll win," her sister said positively.

Mrs. Gray was looking at Daphne. "You don't sound very excited about running for class office."

Lydia didn't give Daphne a chance to respond. "That's because we haven't really gotten started on it. It'll be fun, I promise! We'll work on it Saturday."

She looked so eager and enthusiastic that Daphne didn't have the heart to tell her she wasn't really interested. "Okay," she said.

"Did you join the Creative Writing Club?" Fee asked.

"No. Cassie's got me involved in the Pep Club, and I don't think I've got time to be in any more organizations."

"You know, when I was your age," Mrs. Gray said, "I was an only child, and it was so lonely. I'm glad you've got sisters looking after you like this."

"Have you started working on those announcements for the Pep Club?" Cassie asked. "The first football game's in two weeks."

"She can't work on them tonight," Lydia stated. "We have to start planning her campaign."

"I can't do either," Daphne said. "This girl from my class is coming over to help me with science." She sighed. "I think I flunked a pop quiz today."

"You flunked a quiz?" Mr. Gray exclaimed.

"Oh, dear," her mother said. "Maybe you shouldn't be involved in so many outside activities after all."

Daphne looked at her hopefully.

"It's okay, Mom," Cassie assured her. "Everyone flunks the first pop quiz in science. They make it too hard on purpose to scare kids into studying harder."

Mrs. Gray looked doubtful, but Mr. Gray chuckled. "Yes, I seem to remember that from my school days."

"But you'll have to study harder," Mrs. Gray admonished.

"Oh, I will," Daphne said. "That's why I asked Barbara to come over."

"And no more extracurricular activities," her mother added. "I think you have enough already."

Wistfully, Daphne thought of the Creative Writing Club.

The chime of the doorbell echoed through the house. "That must be Barbara now," Daphne said hastily. She jumped up and ran to the door.

It was Annie. "What's the matter?" her friend asked right away. "You look kind of pale."

"Nothing," Daphne said. "Let's go up to my room."

She remembered something as they climbed the stairs. "Listen, Kimmie's having a party on Friday and we're invited."

"Are you going?"

"Yeah." Daphne flopped down on her bed. "I think Cassie's a little ticked off at me for not sitting with them at lunch. And if I keep on sitting with those other guys, she's not going to be too happy. I guess I'd better go to this party to make up for it."

"For crying out loud, Daphne!" Annie exclaimed. "Are you going to do everything just because it's what your sisters want you to do?"

Daphne was startled by her friend's outburst. "Well, of course not," she said after a few moments. "I mean, this is all temporary. Cassie never stays interested in anything for too long. After a while, she'll stop trying to tell me what to do."

"What about Lydia?"

"Same thing." Daphne hoped she sounded more confident than she felt. "Look, they're my sisters, and they're doing all this for me. I can't just tell them to bug off. My parents think it's wonderful the way they're looking out for me."

Annie looked at her skeptically. Daphne wanted to change the subject. "Can you come to the party with me Friday?"

Annie thought about it. "Can I ask Jerry to come, too?"

Daphne bit her lip. She wasn't about to tell Annie how hard it had been just to get *her* invited. And she had a pretty good idea Kimmie wouldn't think Jerry was the right type either.

"I don't think so," she said slowly. "I mean, it's Kimmie's party, and, uh, I think she's got it all planned for a certain number of people."

Annie frowned.

"Annie," Daphne said quickly. "Remember when you had to go to your cousin's birthday party? That cousin you didn't like? And you wanted me to go with you? I did, didn't I?"

"That was when we were eight years old!" Annie protested.

"It's the principle of the thing," Daphne said firmly. "Friends do things like that for each other."

Annie still looked doubtful. Daphne was trying to think of another good argument when she heard the doorbell ring again. She jumped up.

"There's Barbara now."

Someone had already let her in, and Daphne met her new friend on the stairs. "Hi, come on up to my room. My friend Annie's here, too. Do you mind helping both of us?"

"Not a bit," Barbara said cheerfully. "I figure it's all for the good of science."

For the next hour, Barbara patiently went through the textbook, explaining everything much better than the book did. Daphne had thought she'd be embarrassed to let Barbara see how ignorant she was on the subject. But Barbara was nice about it, never acting like she thought they were jerks for not getting a grip on the material.

"So that's what it means!" Annie shook her head in amazement. "It's actually starting to make sense!"

"Sometimes this stuff can be pretty confusing," Barbara said kindly. "Look, we can't all be geniuses at everything! And don't forget your promise. Next week I have to do an essay for English."

"You'll have your grammar checked twice over," Daphne promised.

"And if Daphne doesn't have time, I'll take over," Annie said.

"Why wouldn't I have time?"

"You're running for vice-president, remember?"

"Oh. Yeah."

"You are?" Barbara looked at her with interest. "What's your platform?"

"Platform?" Daphne looked at her blankly.

"What you're going to do for the school if you win the election."

Daphne gulped. She hadn't even thought about it. Then she grinned. "Maybe I'll abolish science classes."

"Hey, thanks a lot!" Barbara pretended to look offended. "You know, some of us like science!" She paused and looked thoughtful. "But maybe you could get rid of geometry."

"Hey, I'll support that!" Annie exclaimed. "And how about phys ed?"

The girls started laughing as they went through the different subjects.

"Spanish!" Annie suggested. "I hear it's awful."

"English!" Barbara tossed out.

"Hey, no way!" Annie and Daphne yelled in unison.

"What's so funny?" Lydia was standing at the open door.

Annie giggled. "We're trying to decide what Daphne could do as vice-president of the class."

Lydia frowned. "What's so funny about that? Running for class office is no laughing matter! You'd better start taking it seriously, Daphne, if you want to win."

With that, she marched away. Daphne bit her lower lip. She looked at Annie, then at Barbara. They looked like they wanted to keep on laughing, and so did Daphne. But now she felt guilty about it. After all, it meant so much to Lydia. . . .

"I've got to get going," Barbara said. "Hey, are you two going on the field trip Friday night to the planetarium?"

"Why are they having a field trip on Friday night?" Daphne asked.

Barbara looked excited. "There's this comet, and it's

only visible once every ten years. To see it you have to look through this special telescope they have at the planetarium."

"That sounds like fun," Annie said. She turned to Daphne enthusiastically. "Want to go?"

"I can't. Remember? I have to go to that party. And you said you'd go too." She hadn't—but it was worth a try. Daphne felt a little funny talking about the party in front of Barbara.

But Barbara didn't seem to mind. "Well, you can come another time. Maybe in ten years!"

After Barbara had left, Annie turned to Daphne with a grouchy expression. "Gee, I think it would be much more fun to go to the planetarium and see that comet than go to Kimmie's party."

Daphne nodded sadly. "I think so, too. But I have to go, and I don't want to go alone." She looked at Annie pleadingly. "C'mon, Annie. Remember your awful cousin?"

Annie gave a deep, dramatic sigh, but she finally nodded. "Yeah, I still owe you one for that." And then she grinned. "I guess that's what friends are for."

"What?"

Annie's grin widened. "To go to terrible parties together."

8

"Y**OU MEAN** there are going to be boys at this party tonight?" Mr. Gray peered over his coffee cup at Daphne, squinting his eyes as if he was trying to see her better. "Are you ready for that kind of thing?"

His tone wasn't critical or skeptical—just curious, and maybe a little surprised.

"Oh, Daddy," Cassie said in an aggrieved voice. "She's twelve years old! *I* went to parties with boys when I was twelve years old."

"That's different," Mr. Gray murmured.

"Why?" Cassie asked.

But Daphne knew what he meant. Cassie had probably been ready for parties with boys when she was three.

"Whose party is it?" Phoebe asked.

"A girl named Kimmie Lane's giving it. She's in my class."

"She's Barbie's sister," Cassie added.

Phoebe made a face. "And her mother's Mrs. Lane." She looked at their mother. "She's the one who tried to get the books banned from the public library."

"I remember, Fee," Mrs. Gray said. "It was only last month." Her brow furrowed. "I'm surprised she's letting Kimmie have a boy-girl party. She's pretty conservative."

Daphne looked up hopefully. Maybe her mother really disliked Mrs. Lane. Maybe she'd tell Daphne she shouldn't go.

"She wants Kimmie to be popular," Cassie said. "She let Barbie have boy-girl parties last year."

"Isn't seventh grade sort of young for that kind of thing?" Mr. Gray asked.

"Oh, I don't know," Mrs. Gray said thoughtfully. "I used to think that myself. But now I think maybe it's a good idea for boys and girls to begin socializing at an early age. They'll understand each other better and not fall into those silly little games men and women play." She looked thoughtful. "When I was a young girl, I was completely intimidated by boys. They seemed like strange, mysterious creatures I could never be myself with."

Mr. Gray lowered his eyelids and displayed a sinister smile. "I had no idea we were such bizarre animals."

"Oh, Daddy," Cassie moaned again.

"Daphne, you're not eating," Mrs. Gray remonstrated.

"I'm not very hungry," Daphne said. The truth was, her stomach was churning so badly she was afraid eating any food would cause a major disruption.

Cassie turned her attention to Daphne. "It's really nothing to worry about—the boys being there, I mean. Kimmie's only inviting seventh graders, and seventh-grade boys are jerks for the most part. But this will be a good opportunity for you to practice."

"Huh?" Daphne stopped twisting her fork in her spaghetti and looked at her sister.

"Talking to boys. Like I told you before, flirting and all that."

"Flirting—yech!" Fee made a sound to simulate exactly what Daphne was afraid she would do if she ate anything.

"Phoebe, that's disgusting," Mrs. Gray said mildly. Then she turned sternly to Cassie. "That's exactly the kind of silly game I was talking about. Boys and girls don't have to flirt with each other. They can just talk."

Cassie shrugged. "Same difference." She turned to Daphne. "After dinner, I'll give you some tips."

Suddenly the back door slammed and Lydia burst into the room, her books in one arm and a big piece of cardboard in the other. "Sorry I'm late," she said breathlessly.

"Dinner's at six," Mr. Gray said. "It's been at six for many years now, and will continue to be for many years to come. Don't you think it's about time you made a note of that?"

"I know, I know," Lydia said, tossing her books on the kitchen counter. "But I was working on something for Daphne. What do you think of this?"

She turned the piece of cardboard around and held it high for everyone to see. Big red letters, all capitals, proclaimed ALL THE WAY WITH DAPHNE GRAY.

Daphne closed her eyes. Cassie started giggling.

"What's so funny?" Lydia demanded.

"You can't say 'all the way' like that!"

"Why not?"

Even Fee figured out what Cassie meant. "It sounds like Daphne does you-know-what."

Mrs. Gray looked amused. Mr. Gray's expression was one of total consternation. "Uh, Lydia, I don't think that will do at all."

Lydia studied the slogan. "Yeah," she said finally, "I didn't think of that." She tossed the poster aside. "I guess we'll have to come up with something else."

Daphne pushed herself away from the table. "Can I be excused? I want to go take a bath."

"You can use some of my bubble bath," Cassie offered magnanimously.

"Oh, dear," Mrs. Gray sighed in mock despair, "I can see she's going to be just like Cassie and need two hours to get ready for a party."

Daphne didn't argue with her. But it really wasn't the reason she wanted to get into the bathtub. She just wanted to be alone.

Upstairs, she filled the tub using some of Cassie's scented bubble bath and lowered herself gently into the steaming water. At last she was alone with her thoughts.

Why was she feeling so tense? It wasn't the party, not really. She knew she wouldn't have a very good time, not if the guests were all Kimmie's favorite people. She had a pretty good suspicion Kimmie's favorite people wouldn't be hers. But at least Annie would be there, and if there was no one else to talk to, they could talk to each other.

No, it wasn't really the party—it was something else. She closed her eyes and conjured up a picture. Herself—with Lydia pulling on one arm, Cassie pulling on the other. Taking two steps one way, two steps the other. She could pull away, but someone would get hurt. She didn't want to hurt anyone. She just wanted everyone to be happy. . . .

The image disappeared when a gust of air told her she had company. Reluctantly, she opened her eyes. Cassie was putting down the cover of the toilet seat. She sat down and beamed at Daphne.

"This is your first big junior high party! How do you feel?"

"Feel?" Daphne repeated vaguely. "Fine, I guess."

"Good! Now let me give you a few tips on what to talk about. First of all, whatever you do, don't talk about schoolwork."

Daphne frowned. "But that's what we have in common. School."

"Oh, it's okay to talk about *school*," Cassie said hastily. "You can talk about your teachers, and which ones are awful—that sort of thing. But don't talk about the work—unless you're going to complain about it."

Well, she could always complain about science. "What else?"

"With the girls, you can talk about clothes, of course, and the usual stuff like that. With the boys . . . well, it's best to stick to stuff like sports."

"But I don't know anything about sports."

Cassie brushed that aside. "Just ask them what they're going out for. And if they say something like 'Football,' you can always say 'I thought you looked like a football player,' or something like that."

"What if they're not into sports?" Daphne asked. She pictured herself saying something like "I thought you looked like a stamp collector."

"Just try to sound like you're interested in anything they're interested in. And if someone tries to kiss you—"

Daphne sat up in the water. "Kiss me!"

"You never know," Cassie said wisely. "They're only seventh graders, but some of them might be mature. Anyway, it's not such a good idea to let someone kiss you if you've just met them."

Daphne sighed in relief. "Good."

"I'll bet you'd let Rick Lewis kiss you," Cassie said mischievously.

"Cassie!"

"It's okay," Cassie said. "*I'd* let Rick Lewis kiss me."

Daphne tried to imagine kissing Rick Lewis. He might as well have been Bruce Springsteen—that was about how close she'd ever get to him.

"If you do decide to let someone kiss you," Cassie continued, "just don't open your mouth."

Slowly, Daphne sank down deeper into the bath.

"Now, hurry up," Cassie said briskly. "I want to help you pick out what you're going to wear." With that, she left the bathroom.

Daphne tried to picture herself saying "I thought you looked like a football player." She couldn't. Finally, she dragged herself out of the tub, toweled off, and put on her robe.

When she went into her room, Cassie was there looking through her closet and frowning. "I can't find anything in here that looks right. Honestly, Daphne, we're going to have to go shopping."

"Now?"

"Not now, silly." Her sister stepped back from the closet and shook her head sadly. "I can't believe it. You don't have anything to wear."

"What about my green print skirt?"

"Too dressy."

"Jeans?"

"Too casual." Then Cassie snapped her fingers. "I know!" She ran across the hall to the room she shared with Lydia, returning a few moments later with her arms cradling a hot-pink something.

"My new jumpsuit! I haven't even worn it yet. But because this is your very first boy-girl party, I'm going to let you wear it."

Daphne stared at it in distaste. But Cassie looked so pleased with herself that she quickly rearranged her features. "Gee, thanks, Cassie." She slipped into the jumpsuit, and then faced herself in the mirror. It fit okay—but she thought it made her look like a clown.

Cassie clapped her hands in approval. "Perfect! Now, what are we going to do with your hair?"

"My hair?"

"You really need a decent cut. But maybe I could do something with my hot curlers. . . ."

"Look, Cassie," Daphne said hastily, "it's almost seven

now, and we have to pick up Annie. I think my hair's okay just the way it is."

"Wait a minute," Cassie said, running back to her room. She returned with a scarf in various shades of pink. "Sit down," she ordered. Then she started wrapping the scarf around Daphne's head. "This is a very cool way to wear a scarf now, like a headband."

When Cassie had finished, Daphne eyed herself in the mirror again. Now she looked like a gypsy clown.

But Cassie seemed so happy, so proud of her work. "Thank you," Daphne murmured, not wanting to hurt her sister's feelings.

Minutes later on her way downstairs, Daphne met Fee, who eyed her critically.

"Do I look okay?"

Fee cocked her head to one side. "Yeah, I guess so. You look different, though. Not like yourself."

"Who do I look like?"

"Sort of like Cassie."

Well, there were worse ways to look, Daphne thought.

Her mother appeared at the foot of the stairs and caught those last words. "Honey, you don't have to try to be like Cassie. You can have a good time just being yourself."

I don't want to be like Cassie, Daphne wanted to say. Why didn't anyone understand? But then how could they, when she didn't even understand herself?

They left to pick up Annie. Lucky Annie, who didn't have any older sisters, was wearing her usual jeans with a sweater. When she saw what Daphne was wearing, her eyes widened and her nose wrinkled slightly.

"What's that?" she asked, climbing into the backseat.

"It's Cassie's new jumpsuit," Daphne replied glumly. "She's letting me wear it."

"Wasn't that nice of her?" Mrs. Gray said.

"Yes, it certainly was," Annie responded politely. But Daphne, turning around to face her friend, caught the roll of the eyes and the twitching lips. Daphne winked to show her she understood.

"Here we are!" Mrs. Gray announced gaily as they pulled up in front of Kimmie's house. "Do you want me to pick you up later?"

"That's okay, Mrs. Gray, we're going to call my mom and she'll get us."

"Have a good time," she called out to them as they started up the walk. "And be home by ten-thirty!"

The girls waved to her and Annie looked at her watch. "Ten-thirty—you mean we have to stay here three whole hours?"

Daphne giggled. "I'm sure she won't mind if I get home a little early."

Annie grinned. "Like maybe two-and-a-half hours early?"

Daphne recognized the heavyset, orange-haired woman who answered the door. The last time she'd seen her was when she'd stood in front of the town council demanding they ban some books from the public library.

"Hello, girls! I'm Kimmie's mother!"

Daphne smiled politely. "I'm Daphne . . . uh . . . and this is Annie." She had been about to say "Daphne

Gray"—but remembering how Fee had stood up against Mrs. Lane at the town council meeting, she decided not to.

"Come in, come in," Mrs. Lane said heartily. "Everyone's down in the rec room." She pointed the way. "I'm being a very understanding parent and letting you kids have the room to yourselves. But I'm keeping the door open!"

Annie laughed uncertainly.

"That's nice," Daphne murmured. They went down some stairs and found Kimmie waiting at the bottom.

"Hi!" Kimmie said, her greeting directed exclusively at Daphne. She didn't even look at Annie. "I just love what you're wearing!"

It figured—Kimmie was wearing an almost identical jumpsuit, only in turquoise.

Daphne looked at Annie. Her friend didn't seem to mind at all that Kimmie hadn't spoken to her. She was looking around the room curiously.

About fifteen kids were in the room. At one end, the boys had gathered around a table on which sat an assortment of snacks. At the other, the girls were assembled around the stereo, picking through the albums.

"I can't get anyone to dance," Kimmie whispered to Daphne in despair.

Daphne could only smile helplessly. There wasn't much she could do about it—she didn't even know how to dance.

Daphne and Annie wandered over to the girls' side.

One unfamiliar girl was talking loudly. "It's English I hate the most. The teacher I have is so obnoxious you wouldn't believe it."

So Cassie was right, Daphne thought. Complaining was okay. "Which teacher do you have?" she asked the girl.

The girl made a face. "Old lady McBain. She's a real witch."

Daphne and Annie exchanged surprised looks. "We have McBain too," Annie said. "I think she's pretty neat."

From the girl's expression, Annie might as well have said she liked Count Dracula.

"But she makes you talk about all that poetry!"

"We like poetry," Daphne offered.

The girl's expression turned to one of mild contempt. "What are you—brains or something?"

"I think I'll get something to eat," Annie murmured.

Daphne quickly added, "Me, too."

Several girls looked at them in shock. Daphne could feel their eyes on them as they crossed the room to the boys' side.

"No reason they should get to hog the food," Annie whispered. Daphne nodded and tried to look nonchalant as they walked toward the table.

Some of the boys eyed them warily as they approached. One actually looked frightened. Oddly enough, Daphne didn't feel nearly as uncomfortable as she thought she would. The situation was just too silly to take seriously.

Then, one familiar-looking boy, dark-haired and heavyset, swaggered toward them. The other boys watched him admiringly.

"Hey, you're in my history class," he said to Daphne.

Daphne didn't quite know what to say to that. "I guess I am."

His eyes traveled up and down. "That's a pretty wild outfit you're wearing. What do you call that color?"

"Uh, I think it's called hot pink."

The boy snickered and turned to his buddies. "Hey, she's wearing *hot* pink!"

Several other boys started snickering. Daphne blushed furiously. "Uh, excuse me."

She hastily made her way back to the other side of the room, Annie close behind her.

The girls were waiting for them with expectant faces. "What did he say to you?" Kimmie asked excitedly.

"Who?"

"Tommy Barnes! He's *only* the cutest guy in the entire seventh grade! What did he say?"

"Nothing worth repeating," Daphne replied.

Kimmie looked a trifle offended. "Well! I guess you don't have to tell us if you don't want to!"

Annie tried to help out by changing the subject. "Kimmie, where did you go to elementary school?"

"Lakeside."

Annie turned to Daphne. "Isn't that where Barbara went?"

"I think so."

"Did you know Barbara Goldman?"

Kimmie made a face, and two other girls giggled.

"The mad scientist," one of them chortled.

"Oooh, she's such a nerd," the other said.

"Those funny barrettes she wears!"

"And her clothes always look like they're too big on her!"

Daphne's forehead wrinkled. "Maybe she just doesn't care about clothes."

"That's obvious," Kimmie said. "Why do you want to know about Barbara?"

"She's helping us in science," Annie said. "I think she's nice."

"Me, too," Daphne added.

Kimmie and another girl exchanged glances, their lips quivering in funny smiles. Then Kimmie looked at Daphne patronizingly. "Well, don't say I didn't warn you."

"Hey, hot pink—wanna dance?" Tommy Barnes stood there, arms folded, wearing an expression Daphne didn't find the least bit appealing.

"Uh, I don't know how to dance," she murmured. Behind her, she could hear someone giggle.

Kimmie stepped in front of her. "Would you settle for turquoise?" she asked sweetly.

Tommy shrugged. "Okay."

Within a few minutes, most of the kids were in the middle of the room dancing to the music. Daphne noticed a couple of boys still on the other side looking at them. Annie saw them, too.

"I can't believe we turned down a comet for this," her friend growled.

"I know," Daphne replied. "This is even worse than I thought it would be."

The two boys started across the room toward them.

"Daphne," Annie said urgently, "how much longer do we have to stay?"

"How about ten seconds?"

"I'll call my mother."

"Mom says you were home at eight-thirty last night!" Cassie stood at the foot of Daphne's bed in her shortie nightgown, hands on her hips and a look of concern on her face.

Daphne put down the book she was reading. "Was it that early?" she asked innocently. "I didn't notice the time."

"Didn't you have fun?" her sister asked.

"It was okay. . . ."

Cassie looked at her skeptically. "I'll bet you just sat in a corner and moped and didn't talk to anyone."

"I talked to people!" Daphne protested. I just didn't like them, she added silently. But she really didn't want to get into it. Cassie wouldn't understand anyway.

"Look, just because you have a crush on Rick Lewis doesn't mean you shouldn't talk to other boys," Cassie said.

"I know," Daphne said quickly. She jumped off the bed and went to her desk. "I wrote a poem for the Pep Club last night! You know, to get kids to come to the football game," she added, changing the subject and handing a piece of paper to Cassie.

Cassie read silently for a second, and then out loud. " 'Bodies collide in an explosion of energy/While voices signify a similar frenzy. . . .' Daphne, this doesn't even rhyme!"

"Poetry doesn't have to rhyme."

"But this is too . . . too . . . I don't know, like something in a textbook! It should be more like a cheer. You know, like 'Two, four, six, eight, who do we appreciate?'—that sort of thing."

Daphne grabbed the paper away from her. "You're welcome," she snapped, crumpling up the paper and tossing it in the wastebasket.

Cassie stared at her in disbelief. "What's the matter with you?"

Daphne was startled, too. She couldn't remember ever talking to Cassie like that.

"Uh, nothing. Look, I'll write another one, okay?"

Cassie looked at her suspiciously but she only nodded and left the room.

Daphne stared after her. What *was* the matter with her? She'd never felt like this before. All these feelings were churning around inside her—feelings she couldn't even identify. Like she wanted to cry—no, not cry. Scream.

She got up and dressed quickly, then went downstairs. Her father was sitting at the kitchen table drinking a cup of coffee.

"Well, here comes the socialite," he said jovially. "How was the party last night?"

"Okay."

Her father's sensitive eyes narrowed. "Not so great, huh?"

Daphne managed a smile. "I guess I'm not the party type."

Mr. Gray nodded sympathetically. "I can understand that. I'm not the party type myself. By the way, you haven't shown me any of your poems lately. I imagine junior high doesn't leave you much time for creative writing."

Daphne paused as she pulled a box of cereal from the cabinet. He was right—she hadn't been writing much lately. There was that football poem, of course, but that didn't count. Poetry couldn't be written to order.

"I've been pretty busy," she admitted. "Cassie's got me doing all this Pep Club stuff, and then there's the Student Council election."

"You don't seem very excited about either."

What could she say? Luckily, she didn't have to respond.

"Oh, I almost forgot—a letter came for you this morning," her father said, handing her a long envelope.

Daphne looked at the return address. "It's from school." She tore it open and pulled out the letter. It didn't have anything like "Dear Daphne" at the top, so she figured it was some kind of form letter. She read it through quickly.

And then she turned to her father, her eyes wide. "Daddy, it says I have to give a speech!"

"A speech? For what?"

Daphne read aloud, her voice shaking. " 'In order for candidates for class office to present their platforms, assemblies will be held for each class. The ninth grade will gather on Wednesday, the eighth grade on Thursday, and the seventh grade on Friday. All candidates should prepare a ten-minute presentation.' "

She put down the paper and looked at her father in horror. "Daddy, what am I going to do?"

"I guess you'll have to write a speech," Mr. Gray said lightly. But his eyes were concerned.

"But I can't talk in front of all those kids!"

"Daphne, surely you realize that if you want to be class vice-president you'll have to make a speech of some sort." He looked up at the clock. "Honey, I have to go play tennis. But I'll be glad to help you later with this speech."

"Thanks," Daphne murmured, barely hearing him. She was still staring at the letter. She felt hot and cold at the same time.

Now what was she going to do? *You can't give a speech to all those people,* a voice inside stated flatly. *You're too shy—and besides, you don't have anything to say.*

And then Lydia's face flashed across her mind— excited, enthused, so happy to see her little sister following in her footsteps. How could she let her down? Hadn't Lydia had enough disappointment this week?

Daphne thought about the Robert Frost poem, the

one about making choices. But it wasn't any help. That choice didn't carry the risk of hurting your sister.

She stirred her cereal listlessly. Somehow there had to be a solution. But she didn't have the slightest idea how to find it.

9

CASSIE SKIPPED INTO THE KITCHEN. "Mom says we can use her credit card!"

Daphne looked at her blankly. "Her credit card? For what?"

"We're going shopping. I told Mom you had nothing to wear for parties, and she said you and I can go to the mall this afternoon and look around for something. Barbie and Kimmie are going to meet us there at two."

Daphne groaned. Shopping with Kimmie? That was the last thing she felt like doing. "Oh, Cassie, I just really don't feel like shopping today."

"Why not?"

Daphne couldn't think of a good excuse. "I just don't feel like it."

"Oh, Daphne, c'mon! It'll be fun! And the only reason Mom's letting me take her credit card is because I said we'd buy you something. But then maybe I can get something for myself, too, and she'll let me keep it."

Cassie looked so anxious. Daphne felt torn—she didn't want to go, but the expression on her sister's face made her reconsider. Oh, well, she thought—at least shopping might take her mind off writing a speech. "Okay."

"Good! Be ready at one-thirty," Cassie instructed, and left the kitchen.

Daphne looked down at her uneaten bowl of cereal. It was all soggy now. It didn't matter, she wasn't very hungry anyway.

Behind her, the phone rang. She started up to answer but Lydia scampered into the room and grabbed it first.

"Hello? Hi! Can you come? Great, Ted's coming too. I'll see you around two."

As soon as Lydia hung up, Daphne held the bad-news letter out to her. "This says I have to give a speech!"

Her sister read the letter. "Well, of course you have to give a speech! This is a political campaign!" She smiled brightly. "You know, Daphne, this will be a very good experience for you. It's going to help you overcome your shyness."

Who says I want to overcome my shyness? Daphne thought. I've lived with it all my life and it hasn't really bothered me. Why was everyone so keen on changing her?

Lydia was looking at her oddly. "Are you okay? You look funny."

"I'm okay," Daphne said automatically.

"Don't worry about the speech," her sister said comfortingly. "We'll help you write it."

"Who's *we*?"

"Martha Jane and Ted and me. They're coming over this afternoon and we're all going to work on your campaign."

Daphne's forehead puckered. "This afternoon?"

"Yeah, around two. I told you we'd work on your campaign today."

Daphne looked at her blankly. Had Lydia told her that? She couldn't remember. "I'm not going to be here this afternoon. I'm going shopping with Cassie."

Lydia dismissed that with a wave of her hand. "Tell her you can't go. You can go shopping any day. I can't always get people together like this. Besides, the election's a week from Monday."

Daphne didn't respond, but Lydia didn't seem to expect her to. She undoubtedly assumed everything was settled, and she left the room.

Now what? If Daphne had felt trapped before, she felt doubly trapped now. She sat very still on her chair, pulling her knees up to her chest. Strange, unfamiliar feelings kept churning inside of her.

"What are you doing?" Phoebe asked, wandering into the kitchen and opening the refrigerator. She peered inside.

"Nothing," Daphne said drearily. "Everything."

Phoebe managed to tear herself away from the refrigerator for a moment. "Huh?"

"Cassie wants me to go shopping with her at the mall.

Lydia says I have to stay here and work on my class office campaign with her friends."

Phoebe returned to the refrigerator, took out an apple, and turned to face Daphne. "What are you going to do?"

"I don't know. What do you think I should do?"

Phoebe took a bite of her apple. "I don't know," she said, chewing noisily. "Which do you *want* to do?"

That was easy enough to answer. "Neither."

"Then don't," Phoebe replied, and sauntered out of the room.

Daphne watched her sister's retreating figure. She made it sound so easy. She could imagine what Fee would do in a similar predicament. If one of her sisters told her to do something she didn't want to do, she'd say, "Forget it," or something like that. Then there'd probably be an argument, possibly some yelling, maybe even someone getting good and mad.

The thought of it made Daphne shudder. She hated fights, she hated yelling, she hated the idea of someone getting mad at her.

But she didn't want to go shopping. And she didn't want to work on a political campaign.

Suddenly she got up. She went to the window and looked out. It seemed like it was getting cool outside. She went into the hall. She could hear Cassie upstairs talking on the phone, and Lydia in the living room talking to her mother. Very, very quietly, Daphne pulled her jacket out of the hall closet. Then she tiptoed back through the kitchen and out the back door, closing it gently behind her.

She didn't know what she was doing or where she was going. These were brand-new feelings—feelings she wasn't quite sure how to handle.

Well, she had to go somewhere, she reflected a short while later. Slowly, she walked to the village square in the middle of town. She stopped at the movie theater and examined the posters of upcoming features. Then she went into the bookstore, and poked around in the poetry section. She picked up a magazine and began to thumb through it.

"Daphne?"

She turned to see Rick Lewis standing there, and her stomach went into automatic bounce.

"What are you doing here?" she blurted out, immediately regretting her words. Didn't he have a right to be in a bookstore?

But Rick didn't seem to take offense. "I'm meeting some guys at the movies and I got there early. I saw you go in here, so . . ."

Daphne was speechless. Had he followed her into the store?

"What are you reading?" he asked.

Daphne wasn't even sure. She looked at the cover. *"The Poetry Quarterly."*

"You like poetry?"

Daphne nodded, thinking that if she were Cassie, she'd have made a cute remark.

"I don't know much about poetry," Rick said.

"I write a little," Daphne offered, and then blushed. What made her tell him that?

107

But Rick looked impressed. "Oh, yeah? I heard the Creative Writing Club's starting a literary magazine. Are you working on that?"

"I haven't joined," Daphne said. "Yet. I mean, I've been so busy. . . ."

"Well, you said you might drop out of the election. You'd have more time then. By the way, what did Lydia say when you told her?"

"I haven't told her—yet."

There was an awkward silence.

"You have another sister too, right?"

"Cassie."

"Yeah, Cassie. I don't know her very well, but she's pretty different from Lydia, isn't she?"

Daphne agreed, and waited for the next question: "And which one are you like?"

But instead Rick said, "And you're not like either of them, are you?"

Daphne was startled. Was it that obvious? She managed a smile and a shrug.

"I've got an older brother," Rick said, "and we're completely different. He's into sports and I'm not. He likes classical music and I'm into rock. We don't even like the same food."

"You must fight a lot," Daphne said.

"Not really. I mean, we argue, but we don't really fight. Like, he keeps trying to talk me into going out for football next year when I'm in high school. I keep telling him no way, but he keeps bringing it up." He laughed. "He's a hard guy to say no to."

Daphne sighed. "I know what you mean."

"Yeah, I'll bet you have the same problem with Lydia."

"And Cassie," Daphne added.

Rick whistled. "That's rough."

"Sometimes," Daphne said slowly, "it's easier to give in."

"Yeah, I know. Sometimes I feel that way about my brother. But I keep thinking that if I do what he says all the time, I'll be like him. Not that he's a bad guy or anything," he added quickly, "but I wouldn't be me. Do you know what I mean?"

"I know what you mean," Daphne said.

"Well, I've gotta go. I'll see you at school."

"Okay."

For a second he looked like he wanted to say something else.

"So . . . bye."

"Bye," Daphne echoed.

He waved and left the store. Daphne stood there gripping the magazine, his last words reverberating in her ears. He liked her! And she wasn't even trying to be like Lydia or Cassie. She was just being herself—whoever that was.

"Miss, are you planning to make a purchase?" A salesman was looking at her suspiciously. Daphne felt her pockets. She hadn't brought any money.

"Uh, no."

The man pointed to a sign—Please Do Not Handle Magazines Unless You Intend to Purchase Them. Daphne replaced the magazine she was holding, tried to look appropriately apologetic, and left.

Outside, she passed a pay phone. She thought about

calling Annie to see if she was home. But then she remembered she didn't have any money. Well, she might as well just take her chances and walk over there. After all, she didn't have anything else to do. No, that wasn't quite right. She didn't have anything else she *wanted* to do.

A short while later she rang Annie's doorbell, shivering a little as the unseasonable wind cut through her thin jacket.

"Hi," her friend said, looking surprised when she opened the door. "What are you doing here?"

Daphne knew she didn't mean it the way it sounded. But they usually called each other before they visited.

"I have to talk to you. I've got a big problem."

"Come on in." Annie led Daphne into the living room, and Daphne saw to her dismay that her friend wasn't alone. Sitting on the floor surrounded by what looked like little magazines and pamphlets was Jerry, from their English class.

Annie was looking at her curiously, but Daphne pretended not to notice. After all, she couldn't very well talk about her problem in front of someone she barely knew—especially a boy.

"What are you guys doing?" she asked.

"We're trying to work up a plan for the literary magazine," Jerry said. "You know, a lot of schools have literary magazines where they publish stories and poems and sometimes artwork by students. We're looking for ideas."

"Jerry found a whole stack of these magazines from

other schools at the public library," Annie explained. "Ms. Wrenn, the librarian, was going to throw them out the other day when Jerry was there."

"So I asked her if I could have them," Jerry finished. "We thought maybe they'd give us some ideas. Then we could write up a proposal for a magazine of our own and submit it to the principal."

"What a great idea!" Daphne exclaimed. "Can I help?"

"I guess so," Jerry said, looking at Annie. "But it's supposed to be a Creative Writing Club project. Are you still planning to join?"

For a few lovely seconds, Daphne had forgotten the reason she'd come over there. Now it all came back to her and she slumped down on the sofa.

"I want to," she said mournfully. "But I don't think I've got time. I've got all this Pep Club stuff I'm supposed to be doing. And then there's the election. . . ."

Suddenly to her horror she realized her eyes were welling up with tears.

"Daphne!" Annie cried out. "What's the matter?"

Daphne found an old tissue in her jacket pocket and quickly dried her eyes. "I'm okay. It's just that I don't know what to do about my sisters."

She recounted the events of the morning. "Cassie arranged for me to go shopping with her and her friends. And then Lydia told me she'd invited kids over to work on my campaign. If I go shopping with Cassie, Lydia will be angry. And if I tell Cassie I can't go with her, she'll be furious. I feel like everyone's pulling on me and I can't win. I'm trying so hard to make everybody happy. But no matter what I do, someone's going to be angry with me!"

That might well have been the longest speech she'd ever made. And she couldn't believe she was blurting it all out in front of Jerry.

But he looked sympathetic. And Annie put her arm around her. "What are you going to do?"

"I don't know! I'm supposed to go shopping at two o'clock—which is exactly when Lydia is expecting her friends!"

Annie glanced at the clock over the mantelpiece. "Daphne," she said gently, "it's two-thirty now."

Daphne looked at the clock and gasped. "Oh, no!" she groaned. "Now they're *both* going to be furious!"

"Maybe you should call home," Annie suggested.

Those strange feelings started churning inside of her again. And all of a sudden, Daphne knew what they meant. She was angry.

"No!" she said, so vehemently that Annie practically jumped off the sofa. "I'm not going to call them! I'm sick of them pushing me around like this! I don't want to talk to either of them!"

Annie's mouth fell open. For a moment, she looked speechless. Then she clapped her hands. "I was wondering when you'd get around to saying that!"

Daphne looked at her in wonderment. "What do you mean?"

"All the past week, you've been saying 'Cassie says this' and 'Lydia says that.' And it was really getting on my nerves."

"Well, they're getting on my nerves now, too," Daphne said hotly.

"But every time I tried to say anything to you about it, you'd say they were just trying to help you."

"They were!" Daphne exclaimed. "They want me to be happy!"

Jerry looked completely confused. "Then why are you so angry at them?"

Daphne tried to explain. "Because what makes them happy doesn't make me happy." She closed her eyes. "Maybe I'm not really angry at *them*."

"I don't get it," Annie said.

Daphne smiled ruefully. "I think I'm really angry at myself, for letting them tell me what to do."

"If you ask my opinion," Jerry said, "you need to assert yourself."

"Huh?"

"Don't mind Jerry," Annie said quickly. "His father's a psychologist."

"Look at it this way," Jerry said cheerfully, "you're getting for free what most people have to pay a lot of money for."

Daphne almost smiled. "Thank you, Doctor."

"Any time."

Suddenly Daphne realized she was hungry. Not just hungry—starving.

"Annie, have you got anything to eat?"

"Sure! I just made a huge batch of chocolate chip cookies. Want some?"

Daphne nodded vigorously, and Annie went out to the kitchen.

"You know something," she said to Jerry, "you're right. At least, your father's right. I have to go tell them what I'm feeling."

"That sounds good to me," Jerry said. "I'll tell my father to send you a bill."

Daphne couldn't help laughing. "No way! I don't pay for secondhand advice!"

"You know," Jerry said, "I used to wish I wasn't an only child. Now I'm thinking maybe it's okay."

"Having sisters isn't so bad," Daphne said thoughtfully. "I just don't particularly want to face them on an empty stomach."

Jerry considered. "Well, I don't know if that's psychologically sound," he said slowly. Then he grinned. "But it makes sense to me!"

Annie returned with a tray full of cookies. "Like I always say, chocolate can solve any problem. These should help prepare you to do battle with your sisters."

"Absolutely," Daphne said, taking a cookie. Funny— she knew she had a battle ahead of her. But she felt better already.

10

FEELING LIKE A THIEF returning to the scene of the crime, Daphne opened the back door and let herself in. The house was unusually quiet, and she listened carefully for clues as to where her sisters might be. She had an image of them hiding somewhere, lying in wait, ready to pounce. Taking a deep breath, she pondered her alternatives. Should she confront them together? Or take them on one at a time?

And how would they react? Would they be hurt? Devastated? Angry?

She remembered that once when they were little girls, she and Cassie had played dress up with their mother's clothes. Cassie had wanted Daphne to put on some high-heeled shoes, but Daphne hadn't wanted to. They'd felt funny and she'd been afraid she'd fall over in them. Cassie had kept insisting, and Daphne had kept refusing.

Finally, Cassie had gotten angry. She'd stormed out of the room, yelling that she would never play with Daphne again.

But of course, she did.

It occurred to Daphne that maybe she was making a bigger deal out of all this than she needed to. Did she honestly think that Lydia's happiness depended on Daphne being vice-president of the seventh grade? Did she really believe that Cassie's world would crumble if her little sister dropped out of the Pep Club?

Phoebe ambled into the kitchen and opened the refrigerator. As usual, she stood in front of it and examined the food.

Despite her worries, Daphne had to laugh. Phoebe did that a hundred times a day, as if she expected the contents to change magically each time she opened the door.

"Fee, that's the same food that was in there this morning," she said. "Those apples aren't going to transform themselves into a chocolate cake."

"I know," Phoebe said sadly. She took an apple, closed the door, and faced Daphne. "Where have you been? Cassie was looking for you a while ago. Lydia, too."

The chocolate chip cookies Daphne had eaten at Annie's sprang to life in her stomach.

"Where are they?"

Phoebe shrugged. "Guess they went out." Chewing

on her apple, she started to leave the kitchen, but Daphne called after her.

"Fee, when they were looking for me, did you notice anything? I mean, were they mad?"

Phoebe cocked her head and looked thoughtful. "Yeah, come to think of it, they did look pretty steamed. What's going on, anyway?"

Now the chocolate chip cookies were dancing.

"I was supposed to do something with Cassie, and Lydia thought I was doing something with her, and I didn't want to do either of them, so I just left and didn't tell them."

"Oh. No wonder they looked steamed." Phoebe took another bite and chewed pensively. Then she shrugged. "They'll get over it." She sauntered out of the room.

Daphne wandered into the living room. Her mother sat on one end of the sofa with a stack of papers in her lap and a red pencil in her hand. Her father was reading his newspaper and frowning. Daphne perched on the arm of the sofa.

"Hi, honey," her mother said. "Where have you been? Cassie and Lydia were both looking for you."

Before Daphne could reply, her father made a growling noise and glared at the newspaper balefully.

"I've got to take this guy off news and put him back on features," he grumbled. "He did terrific feature stories, but he's lousy at news reporting."

"Why did you assign him to news, then?" Mrs. Gray inquired.

"Because he wanted to be a news reporter. He thinks

real journalists report news. But he's no good at news—
he gets too involved with his stories. Which is exactly
why he's such a good feature writer." He tossed the
paper on the floor. "*Why* don't people just accept
themselves for who they are and what they do best and
stop trying to be something they're not?"

Daphne twisted a lock of hair. "Maybe," she said
tentatively, "because they're trying to be what other
people want them to be."

Her mother looked at her with interest. "That's a
good point. You know, when I was getting ready to
start teaching, Lois Greene—she teaches history—kept
saying I should tell jokes the way she does in class. But
she tells jokes very well, and I don't."

"You're telling me," Mr. Gray snorted.

Mrs. Gray punched him lightly on the shoulder.

"I'm just not suited to funny lecturing," she said.

And I'm not suited for Student Council, Daphne
thought. Or the Pep Club. Or parties at Kimmie Lane's.

"What's up, pumpkin?" her father asked. "You look
like something's bugging you."

Daphne pondered her response. She had to take care
of this by herself. But a little support wouldn't hurt.

"I have to assert myself," she said.

Her parents exchanged glances.

"Can you be a little more specific?" her mother asked
gently.

"I have to tell Lydia and Cassie I can't be like them."

Mr. Gray looked puzzled. "Well, of course you can't.
You're a different person. They know that."

"It's just that they want me to do all the things they do. Lydia wants me to run for class office and be a leader. Cassie wants me to be in the Pep Club and hang out with the popular kids."

"And that's not what you want to do," Mrs. Gray said. "To tell you the truth, honey, I was a little surprised when you said you were running for class office. It didn't sound like you."

"It was all Lydia's idea."

"Why didn't you just tell her no?" her father asked.

"I didn't want her to get mad at me," Daphne said simply.

"And it's the same with Cassie?"

Daphne nodded.

"Oh, dear," Mrs. Gray said. "I was afraid of this. You've got two very strong older sisters, Daphne, and they both like to get their own way."

Mr. Gray looked annoyed. "Well, they shouldn't be pushing you around like this. I'll have a talk with them."

"No, Dad," Daphne said hurriedly. "Thanks and all that, but it's really my fault. I mean, they were only trying to help. I have to tell them."

Her parents exchanged glances again. "How did you get so mature all of a sudden?" her mother asked.

"I don't know," Daphne said thoughtfully. "It's funny. Except for the Creative Writing Club, I really don't know what I want to do. But I know I don't want to do what they want me to do." Her forehead puckered. "I just hope they don't get too mad."

Daphne heard the back door slam and practically jumped.

"Do you want us around when you talk to them?" her mother asked.

Daphne went through a quick mental debate. On the one hand, she knew her parents would take her side. On the other—but there was no time. "No, thanks," she managed, as Cassie burst into the living room.

"There you are!" Her sister's eyes were flashing. "We were supposed to go shopping! I waited and waited for you!"

"I know," Daphne said. "I should have told you. Well, actually, I did tell you. But I guess I didn't tell you hard enough."

"What are you talking about? Tell me what?"

"That I didn't want to go shopping." She gathered her courage, and took the deepest breath she could. "Cassie, I've got to talk to you."

"That's our cue," Mrs. Gray said to her husband, gathering her papers and rising from the sofa.

Mr. Gray looked at her in dismay. "This was just getting interesting!"

But Mrs. Gray gave him a look, and he reluctantly got up. "Try not to spill any blood on the carpet," he advised, following his wife out of the room.

Cassie stared after them. "What's he talking about?"

Daphne had no idea how to begin. She just opened her mouth and let the words come out.

"Cassie, I don't want to be in the Pep Club," she began. But she didn't get much further.

"What?! That's the best club in school!"

"I know, I know," Daphne said, "but it's not for me. And I should have told you before, but I didn't, so I'm telling you now."

Cassie looked aggrieved. "I'm only trying to help you fit in. I just want you to have a good time."

"Cassie, I know that," Daphne started to say, but then she was interrupted again. The back door slammed for the second time, and Lydia burst into the room.

"There you are!"

What was this—instant replay? Daphne waited patiently for what she knew would follow.

"Here my friends come over to help you with your campaign, and you're not even here! Can you even imagine how embarrassed I was?"

"Look, I know, I'm sorry, but—"

"What did you do? Go shopping?"

"Not with me she didn't," Cassie said. "And now she's telling me she wants to drop out of the Pep Club!"

Lydia raised her eyebrows. "Well, that's not such a bad idea. You'll have more time to devote to the campaign."

"Lydia, I don't want to run for class office. I don't want to be seventh-grade vice-president." Was that assertive enough? She took another deep breath. "I'm dropping out of the election."

"Don't be silly," Lydia said briskly. "You don't really want to drop out. You're just nervous because you have to give that speech. It'll be good for you—"

Daphne jumped to her feet. "No, it won't be good

for me! What's good for you isn't good for me! And I don't want to run for seventh-grade vice-president!"

She stopped suddenly. Was that her voice, yelling like that? From the stunned looks on her sisters' faces, she realized it must have been.

"Well, you don't have to get so worked up about it," Lydia said mildly. "I mean, why did you sign up then?"

"*I* didn't sign up," Daphne retorted. "*You* signed me up—remember?"

"Oh, yeah—that's right." Lydia fell silent. "Well, if you really don't want to run . . . how about a Student Council committee?" she asked hopefully.

"I might," Daphne said. "But first I want to join the Creative Writing Club. Then I'll see how much time I have."

"But what about the Pep Club?" Cassie asked.

"Look," Daphne said, "I really appreciate everything you've tried to do for me, both of you. But you're both very different from each other, right? And I'm different, too. And maybe what works for you doesn't work for me."

"But don't you want to be popular and go around with the popular kids?" Cassie asked in bewilderment.

"Huh!" Lydia muttered. "The ones *you* like, Cassie."

"Exactly!" Daphne exclaimed. "Don't you see, both of you? What you want isn't what I want!"

At this Cassie looked a little offended. "What's the matter—aren't my friends good enough for you?"

"Oh, Cassie," Daphne moaned, "that's not what I mean. Your friends are very nice. But I have to make my own friends."

"Oh, well," Lydia said. "If I'm not going to be running your campaign, I guess I'll stay on the newspaper staff. Maybe I can talk that jerk into making some changes."

"If anyone can, you can," Daphne said warmly.

Lydia nodded in agreement. "I'm going to have to get the staff on my side. I'd better start making some calls. . . ." With that, she dashed out of the room.

Daphne couldn't believe it. Lydia wasn't even angry! She turned to Cassie.

"Daphne," Cassie said slowly, "will you do just one little tiny thing for me?"

Daphne regarded her warily. "What?"

"If you ever decide to get your hair cut, will you talk to me about it first? I don't want you getting some crummy cut that will look worse than this one does."

Daphne nodded solemnly. "I will. But Cass, I'm warning you: I'm going to wear my glasses."

Cassie gave her a despairing look. "All the time?"

Daphne nodded.

Cassie shook her head sadly. Then she brightened. "Maybe we can talk to Mom about getting you contact lenses!"

"I don't want contact lenses!"

Cassie threw her hands up into the air. "I give up!" She turned and started out of the room. "But don't forget about the haircut, okay?"

"Okay," Daphne agreed. She knew she wouldn't forget—Cassie wouldn't let her.

Alone in the room, Daphne wandered over to the window. There were still some leaves on the trees—gold, red, and even a few green ones. She took off her glasses. The leaves were blurry, indistinct, their colors blending together. She put her glasses back on. Now she could make out each individual leaf, with its own special shape, its own special color.

Nice, she thought.

11

SEE IF THIS SOUNDS OKAY," Daphne asked Annie, reaching across the cafeteria table to hand her a sheet of paper.

Annie read out loud. " 'I respectfully request that my name be withdrawn from the candidacy list for seventh-grade vice-president. Sincerely, Daphne Gray.' " She handed the paper back to Daphne. "That sounds fine."

Jerry grinned. "I think you've just set a record—the shortest political career in history."

Carefully, Daphne copied the letter again, substituting *membership* for *candidacy* and *Pep Club* for *seventh-grade vice-president.* "There," she said triumphantly. "I'm free!"

"And you can come to the Creative Writing Club

meeting this afternoon," Jerry said. "But go by the office first and tell them to change your identity."

"What?!"

Annie laughed. "That's what they call the cards on file for each student—*identities*. Grades and extracurricular activities and all that stuff are listed on them."

Jerry explained further. "You see, the membership rosters for the clubs have already gone to the office. So you need to have your identity card changed to take off Pep Club and add Creative Writing."

Daphne glanced at the clock. "Okay, I've got twenty minutes till class. I'll go do it now."

She started toward the exit.

"Daphne! Come here!"

Cassie was waving her hands wildly in the air. Daphne made her way over to where her sister was sitting with Barbie and Kimmie.

"Guess what?" she said excitedly.

"What?"

"Let me tell her!" Barbie said. "I was the one who heard it."

"Tell me what?"

"I'll tell her," Cassie said. "She's *my* sister." She beamed at Daphne. "You're not going to believe this."

"Maybe I will if I ever hear it," Daphne replied.

"Barbie was talking to Alison, and she said that Terry Evans told her—do you know Terry Evans? He's in the ninth grade. Well, anyway, he said that—are you ready?"

Daphne could have screamed "I'm ready" but it

wouldn't have made any difference. So she just nodded.

Barbie broke in. "Terry told Alison that Rick Lewis likes a seventh-grade girl!"

Cassie shot her a dirty look before triumphantly finishing. "And we think he's talking about you!"

"A ninth grader," Kimmie breathed in awe, looking at Daphne with new respect.

"What makes you think that?"

"Because I saw Lydia this morning, and she told me Rick was asking questions about you—like, were you still going to run for vice-president, and stuff like that." Cassie sniffed. "Lydia thinks he was only asking because he wants to put you on some committee. But *I* put two and two together."

"Look," Barbie said suddenly. "There he is."

Daphne turned. Sure enough, headed straight toward them were Rick and Lydia.

"Take off your glasses," Cassie pleaded.

But Daphne only pushed them back up her nose.

"Hi," Lydia said. Rick just grinned.

"Hi," Daphne replied. She was aware of Kimmie giggling frantically, but ignored it.

"Lydia says you're definitely not running for office," Rick said.

"That's right. I'm just on my way to the office to put my resignation in the Student Council mailbox."

"You can just give it to me," he offered.

"That's okay," Daphne said. "I've got to get my identity changed. And I've got to put in my resignation from Pep Club."

She heard Cassie let out a mournful sigh behind her, and ignored that, too.

"Then maybe you'll have time to be on the Social Action Committee."

"Maybe," Daphne said cautiously. "I have to see how much time the Creative Writing Club takes."

"Oh, you'll have time," Lydia said quickly.

"Sure you will," Cassie added.

Daphne almost burst out laughing. They'd never give up! But it didn't bother her so much anymore.

"We'll see," was all she said.

"Okay," Rick said. "Hey, are you on your way to the office now?"

Daphne looked at the clock. She still had ten minutes, so she nodded.

"I'll walk you there."

She could feel her sisters' eyes on her as she walked away with Rick. And she suspected they weren't quite sure what was going on with her. Well, neither was she.

It was a short walk to the office—just across the hall and down a bit.

"Maybe," Rick said slowly, "we could get together after school tomorrow and I could tell you more about the Social Action Committee."

"Okay," Daphne said, "but I'm not sure I want to join." She paused. Did she dare say what she was thinking? Why not? "Sure, let's get together."

Rick grinned. "Great!" They were at the office door now. "I'd better go. See ya."

"See ya," Daphne repeated.

No sooner had he disappeared down the hallway than her sisters came tearing out of the cafeteria.

"What did he say?" Cassie asked eagerly.

"We're meeting after school tomorrow," Daphne replied.

"Then you're going to join the committee?" Lydia asked.

Daphne grinned. *"I don't know.* I told him I'd like to get together with him anyway."

Cassie looked shocked. "You told him straight out like that? Daphne, don't you know anything about playing hard to get?"

Lydia rolled her eyes. "Oh, Cass. . . . Look, Daphne, I'm starting a petition. What do you think of the food in the cafeteria?"

"It's terrible," Daphne replied promptly.

"Great! Will you sign my petition?" She produced a sheet of paper.

"Sure." Daphne scrawled her name.

"Now, do you want to serve on the committee to—"

"No, thanks," Daphne said brightly.

"Okay!" And Lydia dashed off.

"What are you going to wear when you meet Rick?" Cassie asked.

"I haven't the slightest idea," Daphne replied. "Probably something like what I've got on."

"Oh," Cassie said. She shook her head as she took in Daphne's plain jeans and shirt. "Too bad." And she went back into the cafeteria.

Daphne went to the office, put her resignation letters in the appropriate slots, and spoke to the secretary.

"Excuse me, I'm changing my extracurricular activities."

The secretary pulled out a box of large file cards. "Name?"

"Daphne Gray."

The secretary flipped through the cards. "I've got a Cassandra Gray."

"No, that's my sister."

The secretary moved the card forward. "Here's a Lydia Gray."

"No, that's my other sister."

The secretary frowned. "I don't have an identity for you."

Daphne was startled. "What did you say?"

"Oh, wait a minute, here it is. It was stuck, caught in the middle between these two." She pulled it out and smiled.

"Your very own identity."

That's me, Daphne thought. Caught in the middle. But breaking free.

With my very own identity.